Violets & Delphiniums

Poco

TO EVERYONE I'VE LOVED BEFORE

For anyone who ever wondered, 'what if.'

For my dear family and friends, whose love I simply couldn't do without. Thank you.

To KP, Skye B & Ziggy, my dudes.

To my adored hometown of Leamington Spa & it's many special souls.

With much love and thanks to artist SP Williams who very kindly donated her artwork to this project. Isn't it beautiful!

Finally, this book was completed in Lockdown 2020. May peace, health and happiness not be far away.

Poco x

ABOUT THE AUTHOR

Poco is a pseudonym,
because if I'm going to write a novel, I think I deserve
some fun and mystery along the way.
Poco was my adored first cat, she was black and white and
kind and gentle. She used to come on holiday with us. She
was also pretty tough.
I've written quite a few drafts of quite a few novels, this is
the first one I've actually completed, and I'm thrilled to
actually get this far!
I'm a content creator, writer and photographer by trade.
And although I've been published many times, this is my
first novel. It means an awful lot.
I completed this in Lockdown 2020. Suddenly I had more
time on my hands and really needed to escape to other
worlds.
Thank you so much for reading this book, my next novel
will be published later this year.

Peace, love and custard creams.

You can find me on Facebook @Poco_author

OUR TALE BEGINS ONE
DARK & STORMY NIGHT
IN LEAMINGTON SPA…

CHAPTER 1

Creeping and swarming and spinning and suuuucking. Boldly squirming hips-a-swirling.

Damp rust seeping and suppurating through the walls made it look as if the house was bleeding. Veins of blood red, dirt brown, pleuritic green and poisonous inky black swam up in glistening dark corners, just waiting to devour the house in its entirety when no one was looking.

Tenacious in its task, it was slowly absorbing the plaster, choking the walls with a stark ferocity until they found it hard to breathe. Spluttering, gasping and palpitating until eventually they had to succumb to its inevitable dull dank mercy.

Bathed in indignity. Bathed in ultra-violet. Bathed in the beginning of the end.

The 'a little past their best' dusty and squalid, oldest of old oil lights flickered tiredly and erratically in a not so stately ruin; full of faded magnificence and missed opportunity in their worn, yellowing, ever so sad, ever so grey and weeping tear-stained holders. A dropped pearl hung by the thinnest of threads and was a solitary survivor, suspended in space and floating in the ether, unloved and uncared for. Mother had preferred the kinder glow of oil and candle light.

'It illuminates rather than dissipates darlings,' and was dismissive of 'the electrics,' as she called them.

'What folly, what madness, spectres in our midst; no good will come from it.'

Candle wax now pooled under the candelabra on the desk whilst Guy absent-mindedly picked at it, gathering great clumps of the stuff under his well chewed, stained and nervously bitten fingernails. As soon as he had a big piece he held it under the flame and watched it return to the fire, dissolving to nothing and regaining its freedom. He liked the way it melted over his fingers. It hurt a little bit and burnt his skin pink. It was something, rather than the mind-numbing abyss of empty and never-ending nothingness. He let it burn. He delighted in the sting.

The clock ticked, the fingernails clicked, dry lips were licked, wax nicked and picked; the walls bled, and the lights flickered and sputtered in the languorous listless lounge of the white house with the green front door. Yet Harriet Leighton was oblivious to any such magical, enchanted activity and sat tapping her shiny boot black T-bar shoed foot on the floor.

'Tip tap tippity toe.'

Anything to make some noise that would fill up her ears other than the blood gushing and slowly sloshing deafening nothingness - anything to release the boredom and palpable silence of watching her brother lost in his thoughts again.

'Bloody hell, come on, COME on' screamed Harriet in her head to the silent room, to time immemorial and to their faltering universe. She dug her nails into the palm of her hand which she found considerably satisfying.

They had already sat like this for over an hour, killing time, deliberately slaughtering the seconds until he slept. It was a daily occurrence, a duty for them both, bound in an unspoken love and urgent need to belong, that no end of staring into space could destroy, no matter how tedious it could seem on dark and terrifically dull nights like tonight.   They were family.

Harriet, for her part was always astounded at how fascinating candle wax could be to another human being. It was always the same and, on some days, if she remembered in time, she came into the room early and made little grooves with the side of a knife on the edge of the candle so that it would drip and drop and drizzle more effectively. He never said if he knew that she did this, but she didn't do it for praise. She did it to give him a few moments of interest, even if it was totally nonsensical to her. She had to give him something. It was a gracious act from one that loved ferociously.

Finally, FINALLY! The clock struck 10.00, it boomed in their heads − an explosion that would require immediate action. That action was a divine pause. Neither of them moved for a moment, an exquisite moment that was by far their favourite of the whole damn day. It lasted a second, was imperceptible and was blissful. Then they acknowledged the interruption and caught each other's eye.   Harriet saw a base, always there, always bloody there, sadness and a momentary reprieve in equal measure in his face, and Guy saw boredom pass and a look he recognised, blessed relief, follow quickly into his little sister's eyes. He smiled.

'It's time now little bird.'

Harriet got up and walked over to the cabinet, he was always so punctual. He would never allow her to the cabinet before the clock struck, not even at 9.59. It was as if he was holding on, counting until the moment came and controlling any urges he had left. It felt terribly important that the time was observed.

'One two buckle my shoe, three four, open the door.'

She took the key, on its delphinium blue ribbon out of her pocket and unlocked the door.   It always made her smile that he chose such a pretty colour. It wasn't a standard one from the catalogue, he had the shop order it in especially. Again, it seemed important that this was observed, and a new ribbon would arrive each month, so it always looked vibrant and cheerful. She had found dozens of the old ones plaited together in the bureau drawer. Tons of delphinium and azure blue in various shades of use which she found beautiful.

'Nearly there now.'

She smiled at him as she reached for the medicine in the brown unmarked bottle, which was also not standard or off the shelf, and was delivered by an unknown hand once a month. Feeling the cool glass under her skin raised her spirits no end. In moments he would be in another place, unaware of what was happening in this big old crumbling house.

She poured a little of the medicine into his special sherry glass which no-one was allowed to touch, even to clean. She would see him at the sink the next morning delicately soaping and massaging it like a piece of the finest crystal rather than the cheap Woolworths glass it was. Only he could return it ready for the next evening. It was another part of the ritual. Harriet continued with the task at hand and topped the medicine up with a little Cointreau, which was the way he liked it. He'd grown accustomed to it, all those years before in France and in his more lucid moments was rather protective of it and all it remembered.

The delicate citrus aroma transported him to that little square by the church, surrounded by orange trees; the blossom in the summer months was just intoxicating on the breeze. A perfect contrast to his bitter sharp coffee which he'd drink boiling hot, hot enough to burn his throat even when the sun made his cheeks quite red.

'I'm alive.' He said to no-one in the room, which was now tingling with his anticipation.

He licked his lips at the memory, it was such a tonic. He made a mental note to order in some more. At the department store, Burgis and Coleman, where they placed their household list, a man, wearing white gloves had to descend to the cellar where they kept it cool until it was required. It was very expensive and considered an eccentric order by those, who wondered why Scottish whisky would not suffice, wondered how they could afford it, wondered if the Leighton's still had the family wealth. Wondered but did not understand or care to.

'Some things need no wonderings, they simply are and need no questions. It is, it is, it is.' Guy was fond of telling his sister as a particular or interesting action took him. Harriet smiled to reassure him. It was his truth and they allowed it. Complicit in every way.

Despite it being such a precious commodity, at 10pm Harriet was allowed to touch the bottle, but he observed her carefully, watchful in case she spilt a drop. Her hand always trembled a little in case she did, but she never had. This was why she was so good at assisting him. His little sister seemed robust enough not to shake too much and kind enough not to judge and to indulge his strict schedule.

'Ready?'

Harriet always asked and never waited for the response, she knew the answer. She closed the door and locked the cabinet, returned the key to its place in the family cash box, which was also locked, and that key kept by Harriet. It was then put into a locked drawer and the key to that given to Guy. He wanted to make it difficult to access the medicine and the brandy together. He was afraid if they weren't secure, he may give in to temptation and then the days preceding the nights would also be lost to him. Once he was satisfied that he would be safe, and they were protected did he nod to his sister. Only then did she walk towards her brother.

'Gently, slowly dear.'

She knelt beside him and put the glass to his grey lips. He always coughed after his first sip, so she paused until he had regained himself before she tipped the glass up again. The moisture appeared in his rheumy reddened eyes and he smiled at her for the last time that day.

'It is, it is, it is.'

Sleep came quickly after the last drop of the sweet viscose liquid had slipped, slid and slithered down his congested throat. Clogged up with memories and incident. The tears came now freely, and he shut his eyes and felt no shame as he bade his sister, 'Goodnight.' She took his hand until she knew he was lost to her.

'Top notch Harry.' he mumbled.

'Sleep well.'

Tick tock, tickety-tock Harriet was now on the clock. She quickly finished her routine; candles to blow out, oil lamps to turn down to just a flicker. Blanket over his legs, sneaky sip of medicine she'd squirreled onto a spoon, double check medicine bottle locked away. Key in pocket. Kiss Guy on the forehead. She smiled as she finally closed the door, her night had just begun.

In the hallway all was silent, the atmosphere shifted as the house took its sigh of relief and relaxed as its guardian slept. More damp took its opportunity and began to grow in hidden corners and Mother smiled at her from the portrait in the hall.

'Goodnight Mother.'

'Don't let the bed bugs bite' she replied.

CHAPTER 2

She took the stairs to her room two at a time and threw off the dainty; 'Oh isn't it just the most delightful,' cardigan covered in little rosebuds. It had been a terribly expensive yet appropriate present from her siblings last Christmas, but after her duties were complete she often clandestinely swapped it for something that felt a little more Harriet.

Her concealed pleasure was secretly hidden at the back of the wardrobe. Black silk, liquid, languish-ly, water-falling, tumbling over the shoulder top, which clung luxuriously in all the right places. Harriet had taken a knife, not just to the candle in the parlour but to the drawer too and opened the cash box to find more money than she could have possibly imagined. Guy would not miss a teeny-weeny little bit and she told herself he wouldn't begrudge her some of it anyway. She knew he would not notice or would imagine he had done it himself during his night terrors. A little confusion could help at times.

'Steal, stash silently and don't stumble darlings,' said an ever present, all knowing Mother.

A sudden sound above her made her aware that she wasn't the only one awake in the house. The dragging, hauling and heaving noises of furniture being shifted around meant they were in the loft space again, far too preoccupied as always to bother about her. This was, as always - a terrifically good thing.

A hairline crack appeared in the ceiling after a particularly heavy bang, sending a dart of the bloodiest rust unveiling hidden damp riches.

'It always wins in the end,' said Mother, who was fond of telling her children what a constant battle it was to keep the white house on an even keel.

'Exhausting poppets, free yourselves.'

Harriet sighed and tousled her short bob haircut, which had only been tidied up recently since she'd hacked it all off herself. Dear Guy had disapproved of the idea, thought it wasn't 'proper' for a young lady:

'Especially not for a Leighton girl.'

He was trapped in a past that was trying very hard to be forgotten.

And he had never really understood any Leighton girl, he had ever met.

Harriet, true to form, was not to be quashed so easily.

'That girl has too much gumption.'

She'd stolen the kitchen scissors from their help and friend, Greta and had taken matters into her own hands. Biting her lower lip in concentration and determination, it was goodbye childhood plaits and hello to Jean Harlow bob. If she could also have dyed it peroxide blonde like her heroine she would have done, but she needed to pick her moment and introduce changes one at a time, bit by bit.

'Slowly, slowly, catchy monkey,' as Mother used to say. Best to strike when they were otherwise absorbed in some other pressing matter. Of which there were many in the big white house with the green front door.

She admired her handiwork nonetheless. Admittedly it had been rather helped by the local hairdresser whom Guy had sent round to tidy it all up after the event. It may not quite be from the studios, but she had the most fashionable haircut of any of her friends. She liked the way it made her stand apart from them, it felt terribly sophisticated and grown up.

'Who does she think she is?'

'She's not even twenty, it's disgraceful.'

'I bet she kisses all the boys.'

She loved to overhear such comments. She wasn't upset or cross, she would simply smile adoringly at her attacker which seemed to wrong foot them.

'Don't you just love it, I know you do, almost as much as me.'

'So modern, so vogue.'

Most importantly, she liked the way her new haircut exposed her neck which was perfect for lips to touch. It made the hairs stand up on her arms just thinking about it and she felt a pressing in her stomach.

She took kohl out from a pair of socks which were hidden at the back of the drawer and drew thick black lines on the rim of her violet eyes and a little bit up the side. At a glance she resembled her brother, the lost soul in the faded drawing room below her; although his dark eyes were all his own creation drawn from medicinal nights and, hers were 'divine' as someone once said, somewhere on the breeze.

She dug around and pulled out a little pot of rouge which she had taken from mother's dressing table a lifetime ago, dabbed some on her cheeks and a little of the raspberry red on her lips as was the fashion. Harriet didn't waste time, in less than ten minutes she was ready. As she quietly shut the door she remembered to leave the light on, just in case anyone passed by. Harriet giggled inside knowing they were oblivious to her night time wanderings.

Passing Mother's portrait in the hallway, they exchanged knowing looks.

14

'Darling girl, you glow.'

The cool glassy night air delighted her, it was fresh on her face and she could smell excitement in the atmosphere. As soon as she shut the green front door of the big white house she felt free. Freedom was greedily tasted and tonight it was a heady mix of fire smoke and lime trees. She licked her lips and ran her tongue over her teeth.

'I'm alive.'

The house continued on its relentless journey, alive, alive, oh!

She ran the few metres to the park gate. Past grand old Harrington House, with its turrets and solemnity. They were forever trying to force her to make friends with the boy that lived there, but he was a cold fish and Harriet had enough of those at home.

Autumn had begun in earnest; the leaves had started to change and it was dark and chilly. This meant that they locked the gates earlier than just a few weeks ago when she had sweltered in the sun. The big old heavy padlock was trying to bar her entrance, but that was of little consequence. Deftly she scaled the wrought iron railings and was over in a jiffy. She laughed again; it was just so terribly easy. Harriet loved the Regency detailing on the gates, everyone did. People travelled from other towns to admire Leamington's beautiful stucco buildings, elegant parks and wrought iron, but best of all the intricate pattern meant that there were little footholds all over the gate.

'Tah-dah.'

Unbeknown, her sisters watched expressionless from the skylight of the big white house with the green front door, their white hair illuminated by the moon.

'It's that time.'

'Noted dear.'

The park was quiet, the wind occasionally rushed

through the trees and the scent of late flowering buddleia caught her breath, intoxicating her. The clock tower chimed the half hour, 10.30, right on cue.

The night and Harriet were young

CHAPTER 3

They ate breakfast in silence as they always did. Greta had prepared scrambled eggs, which was served on Mother's duck egg china plates at the twin's insistence.

'We use the best because beauty is in our veins. To not do so would be callous to our sensitivities.' Mother instructed her girls, much to her husband's infuriation.

A delicate posy of violets sat in a Wedgewood vase with Greek twirling and turning goddesses. Harriet and Guy were subdued due to the night's activities. As Harriet stumbled in at the early hours she could hear her brother pacing in his room calling their names over and over again. It was always the same.

'Cheri.'

'Unity, I'm here, don't be scared.'

'Mother leave us now.'

The holy trinity of terror for her brother.

The twins however were their usual alert selves and smiled with sparkling white teeth, occasionally at one another, as they passed each other things without having to ask first. Butter and marmalade and toast went between them, each knowing what the other wanted without even looking at it.

Their expressions were cold and stony and stunningly beautiful towards their siblings, which was par for the course. It made Harriet dislike them a little more with every bite she took. She even bit her tongue after a particularly angry bite and could taste the iron rich blood mixing with the eggs. It made her feel quite nauseous.

'You look tired today Harriet.'

'Didn't you sleep well?'

'You have dark circles under your eyes again.'

Harriet barely responded to her sisters and grunted at them, she really must remember to make sure all of the kohl had been rubbed from her eyes. Guy reached over and squeezed her hand.

'Ahh Harry, such a help again last night.'

'I think you look very well as always, but maybe you need some more eggs to get you up and running, come on little bird.'

Guy took his sister in and thought she looked peaky, was he asking too much of her?

Greta as usual was gamely being cheerful and tried to appease the chilly breakfast proceedings. She loved them all really despite their individual little ways. And she did indulge Harriet somewhat, but she had been so troubled when her mother passed on and she first met her. She needed an older woman's love and guidance and she doubted her older sisters were suited to the role.

It was true, Harriet had lost her way a little, but many of the young people had. Much of the country had.

'Here liebling.'

'English! Remember Greta, at all times,' said Charity with a smile that was quite bewitching and ice-blue eyes that didn't change a jot.

To Harriet's despair more eggs were put on her plate. She tried her best to gulp them back but could still taste the iron seeping into her throat and had to have the cool congealed lumps of egg with lots of sugary tea to wash it all away.

'Thank you Greta. Harriet there is still a depression on,

so many are hungry and as a Leighton girl we must be upstanding. We have a certain reputation and you must not waste the food.' And an icy beam of a bared teeth smile fell full force from Grace.

'Quite right dear, I'll sit here and watch you until you finish them,' said Charity, squeezing her little sister's arm until red rings formed.

Watching, inspecting, examining.

'Where would I be without your keen observation, Charity?' muttered Harriet and she instantly regretted it as the twins smiled, satisfied with each other. They did seem to enjoy getting under each other's skin.

Greta sighed, those girls! They rarely seemed to miss an opportunity to take Guy's well-meaning thoughts into defensive action. Like the eggs it was served up on a plate and rather cold.

Much as she respected the Leighton twins they weren't by any stretch of the imagination nurturing or especially generous. At eight years older than Harriet and ten years younger than Guy, they were isolated by circumstance. But this wasn't their fault, as Greta had read up on the works of Viennese doctors and felt that maybe the trauma of losing their parents had made them a little emotionally cold to stop anyone hurting them that much again.

Greta liked to think that people and things had a reason. She felt dizzy at any singularity that suggested the opposite.

And she did not like to feel dizzy.

Grace had found the book of course and had thrown it on the open fire.

'Utter clap-trap.'

Greta was such a sympathetic soul, she only wanted to see the good, despite this cold and peculiar house which she tried to call home. On cue, a bit of precarious plaster became dislodged and she watched as a thin line of rust took its chance and seeped and snaked hissing down the wall.

'Dearie me', said Guy as he brushed the dusty shard from the table and the dust mixed with the congealed remnants of egg. Harriet felt sick.

Greta did worry about Guy; he was a difficult man at times. And was told much changed after his time on the front, by Audrey, who was one of the few people who shared news at Betty's corner shop. Audrey happily told everyone that he left a happy, loving boy, 'always so close to his mother.' And returned a shell of his former self.

'He fell in love in France with that la de da woman, Cheri and it's her name he calls over and over again in the Newbold Arms when he's *tired* and as for the little girl, well it was all so very tragic.'

'This is what happens when you up-sticks, wouldn't have happened with a local girl.'

Audrey had frustratingly failed to cure him, despite her obvious charms and repeated attempts to soothe him. She was a little suspicious of this beautiful small foreign woman, but she rationalised that Greta was a Hun and 'My Guy' would have none of that.

'Yes Harry, do finish the eggs, I've had quite enough to eat, and the protein will be good for you.' Shaking hands passed the toast and butter towards Harriet too.

Guy had returned from the war, all those years ago and had survived, but as each and every survivor knows, there are consequences to surviving and you never truly escape anything.

The house understood and for once Mother was quiet from her portrait in the hall.

Rather, the torment and the wounds live with you forever, which is your cross to bear, your reward and your lucky escape. It's still there in the corners and it is awfully patient, it's in no rush.

On cue, another bit of plaster landed in the eggs and

Harriet sighed.

The scars themselves can of course turn septic if not looked after properly and unless you are quite meticulous (and who can be that bothered, after everything else) the poison runs too deep and the very thing that you originally escaped takes its inevitable toll and claims the reward which at first it was denied.

Eager and excitable, it snaps and snips at your ankles until it tastes second blood. You are just waiting for it to happen, everyone around you is, and it's claustrophobic and no one can breathe properly. And you are one of the silent many that know this truth.

So, there are violets and there are eggs and there are pretty china plates.

It frightens, terrifies, preoccupies and rips at the very fibre of your being. You carry on. Everyone else does.

'Have some extra butter too Harriet dear.'

This was Guy's lot, nothing or nobody had rescued him this time round. They had all thought him suitably recovered as was often the case in circumstances such as his. 'A little war trouble perhaps.'

He was just a little changed maybe, quieter and a little strange which was all so understandable, there was nothing wrong. And 'we all have our quirks,' as Mother often noted.

'Whatever doesn't kill you makes you stronger.' Eh my boy, said Mr Leighton, who knew all about quirks of character.

Or so everyone said, another little white lie to make it easier for everyone else. And so, he chose the tempting silky comfort of his dear friend alcohol and his special cousin medicine, which offered him some relief and was kind to him. He needed a kindness. And it was his little sister he chose to assist him. He knew she understood.

'There eat up, my sparrow.'

And Harriet was only half way through the spectacle that was breakfast.

CHAPTER 4

Greta also knew all about surviving and not through any Austrian book she had read. It had happened some years ago now. Her husband had gone to sort out some of their paperwork in the City. She'd waved him off on the train in the morning with a cheese sandwich, cheese taken from the big white house as her own supply had run low. She told herself that they wouldn't miss it and besides he needed the sustenance more than the family.

'Auf weidershein mein liebling'

'Wir sehen sie uns bald liebling'

She was pleased afterwards that they had had this little exchange; pleased she had kissed him, and it also somehow seemed important that he had had something to eat before the event and pleased she had waved him off. If her memory served her well, it was the 7.50 to St Pancreas, via Oxford.

Greta rationalised that it had been about 7.42 when she had last felt those warm lips on hers. And now whenever she caught that time on the clock, she squeezed her dead husbands' hand and sometimes if she was very tired, she felt he squeezed it back.

Afterwards she'd cycled back to the house and prepared breakfast on those duck egg blue plates and now whenever she saw those damn plates she was transported back to that day. But the twins were insistent that they be used every morning. 'It has been that way since Mother shook off her mortal coil and will continue.' She didn't expect that they realised that a little bit more of her died each and every breakfast time looking at that china set. But she didn't grumble, didn't want to complain.

The twins smiled their supersonic smile.

They had looked after her, given her the room at the back of the house. It had been cold and cheerless with just an iron bedstead and water jug, but she had transformed it with herbs and flowers from the garden and had knitted herself a cheerful little blanket, which three years later was just about big enough to cover her single bed. Besides it gave her a project, something to do in the evenings and for that she couldn't thank them enough.

Milly, so named by Harriet, from 'Milly Molly Mandy', the pet cat had taken up residence with Greta. Pleased to at last find a calm person to sit with, someone who liked a cuddle and someone who would talk to her. They made a good pair, refugees from some of the strange going-ons in the house which Greta assumed were English things as they could be sometimes rather eccentric, and wasn't that what the British were renowned for?

Greta had brought up one of the little bowls from the kitchen which she filled with fresh water every day and the cat wasn't fussy with the kitchen scraps and the little extra, which she deliberately cooked. It was important to her to have someone that relied on her, it gave her some purpose and some hope.

It had been later in the day when she heard. She was in the kitchen trying to clean a pair of Guy's trousers onto which he'd spilt some of his special brandy, which for some reason was harder to clean than the normal stuff, stickier, thicker. She remembered Guy calling her into the front room, in itself quite an unusual act. She hurried, her sleeves still rolled up from the soapy suds.

'Can I get you anything Mr Leighton?'

She knew something was up when she saw the policeman standing by the window, she just knew. Greta couldn't really remember being told, just remembered Guy leading her to the sofa and her concern that her dress might not be too clean after being in the kitchen all morning.

They tried to hide the newspaper the next day, but she'd found it in the fire grate and seeing it in black and white made it real for the first time. So, she got up and took to her seat in the kitchen for a whole day without moving once, before little Harriet came and got her and put her in the small room at the top of her house, which had been her home for the last five years. Greta never found out what happened to the bedsit she had shared with her husband. She didn't care at the time and was incapable of doing or considering anything. She regretted it now, there were some photos she would have liked to have seen again.

The white house with the green front door had acquired another inhabitant.

Greta hadn't left the room initially for three weeks, with only Milly for comfort and Harriet bringing her odd plates of food, which her teenage self, thought constituted a meal. It wasn't unusual to have custard and crackers for example or sardines with an apple. It didn't matter because she rarely ate what she was given. Everything made her feel quite sick. One day a bottle of brandy was outside her door and she knew that Guy had left it. There was a little violet on the tray with it which she thought was kind. It had helped her get a bit of sleep and strangely given her more of an appetite and slowly she began to regain her strength.

So, this was her family now, they had cared for her as

best they could, which admittedly was rather haphazard, but maybe this was some of their Englishness. They were not much more than children themselves, parentless and eternally so. Harriet and even Guy had sat with her occasionally, even if they were usually 'lost' in their own worlds, but she loved them for trying. Especially Harriet, who would read her the adventures of Pooh Bear or her favourite Alice in Wonderland. Childhood books that were still somehow relevant.

The twins of course didn't like sickness and wanted to shut it all away. Greta later found out that they never even ventured up to the top floor in those first few weeks, fearful or disgusted, she couldn't decide which.

'Sickness travels dear, it gets under one's skin; we must not be tainted.'

They were so very disturbed that even painting had ceased as they couldn't bear to go to their studio. Although it was at the other end of the landing, she was dangerously close for them.

'Cleanliness is next to Godliness.'

Anyway, despite this, she had stayed; she had nowhere else to go.

He was killed in Trafalgar Square, when a heated group of jobless marching veterans, infuriated by the depression heard him speak; heard his German accent as he helped a child up after falling over. They took a knife to his back and he ended up in the fountain.

His blood spiralling and looping forever upwards in the watery spray. No doubt it made a colourful and vibrant display. They didn't tell her about the cheese sandwich they'd found squished up and uneaten in his pocket.

They'd left when life in Germany became difficult. In 1930, National Socialism was on the rise, the leader of the party was out of prison and the country was struggling. Henrich was a writer and the authorities disapproved of his 'left wing' tone and they had no choice. They had managed to escape just before a mob arrived at their apartment and fled Berlin in the early hours. They managed to get across the border and they'd been hiding out in France for a while. Henrich wrote for a while from France, which told the world about Germany and how it was destroying itself, spoke of the new National Socialists and chartered their rise to prominence. It had meant it was unlikely that they would ever return home. They would become one of the many missing people, who were there one day and then not seen or heard of again.

After their time in France, they wanted to come to Britain where Henrich had family. They hoped hostilities may have calmed between the nations all this time after the Great War. They still wanted to come to the country that had slaughtered their kin, it offered a new start.

After a short time in Birmingham with Henrich's family, they saw an ad for help in Leamington Spa, close enough to the family but far enough away to build their own life at the same time.

It had been difficult; they were not popular at all and were met with suspicion wherever they went. Everyone had lost somebody or something along the way, little had been great about the Great War, everyone was suffering. The people they met didn't know about the pain they had gone through too, all that they had lost. The side they had so obviously chosen the home they could never return too. The people didn't care and didn't try to understand, they couldn't because they had lost too much. Their brothers, sons, husbands, uncles, fathers murdered, most by the enemy, some by their own side. So much anger, pain and loss. The war had taken too much of a toll for there to be any sympathy.

'The only good German is a dead German.'

At first it used to make her cry, she had stopped that now, but it still hurt a bit. She had found her place and the family to their credit had defended her. Uncle William had employed them straight away, they were very cheap which was incredibly appealing. And Uncle liked the fact they were Germans, had heard about, 'this new chap, Hitler, sounds like a jolly good fellow, clean things up a bit eh.'

The family were broken and she as much as the others. The children were grown up, just Harriet, a wayward teen then, who had just lost her mother needed care. At least that's what they were told, it soon became apparent that Harriet was the least of the problems.

Yet she was cheerful in spirit and made the most of each day. She felt she was only in waiting until she could go to Henrich and in a strange way that made things easier and in her own way she was content. They were her family now and she theirs.

Mother smiled.

Das ist gut ya

CHAPTER 5

It was all very different before the war for the Leightons, certainly for the twins and Guy when their parents had been alive. The house was spic and span, as were they.

Harriet was a war child, born into madness. But there always has to be one.

'Mummy's little surprise,' said Mother often.

Mr George Ansel Leighton, upstanding member of the town, royal don't you know. Unquestionably and irrevocably correct at all times, a true Victorian, born in the age of the empire, with a young family he treated as the inhabitants of his own personal kingdom.

He was a banker by trade, although the job was unnecessary really. The Leightons came from a long line of wealthy middle classes and 'work' was not a requirement. In fact, it was a little discouraged, but George had a conquering nature and after he received his first work assignment his father christened him 'the pioneer,' a status which he enjoyed immensely.

Mr Leighton enjoyed business, he felt it gave him purpose and gave him the chance to disappear to the city and his club when he felt the need. In the opium dens and in the East End down by the river he could forget all sense of the moral family man and did so frequently. He thought it was his just dessert after the hours spent toiling in the boardroom.

'Beer, bollocks and buggery,' his colleagues would cheer after 6pm and it was important to join in with the chaps.   'Supporting the team is most important, Guy.' He would tell this to his son, whom he hoped one day would join him in the realm of men.

No one ever dared to disagree with George and the house kept to its part too and was terribly well-behaved. There was no dust. There was no damp. Not a flicker, or a licker. Solid, firm – just like him.

In Crown Wharf one evening he fathered a child he never met, never even knew about. It was only after his death and the woman came to the house with the child, which was undoubtedly his, the eyes were the same and the hair as white as the twins; that the family found out at all. Uncle dealt with it. Mother was far too bereaved.

'William, I feel a little weak, I'm afraid you must really step up, your sister is overcome.'

William sighed and would be heard to mutter 'bloody George' under his breath. Despite his sister's obvious weaknesses, he found himself frequently doing as she bid. She was a woman after all; 'bloody, bloody, George.'

'Darling Chubbs,' his sister would say and he was rather fond of her attention.

The slight sea change and the barometer swirled. Finally, the house could dance a little.

George Ansel Leighton was only 42 when he died forcing his troops out from behind the trenches. The fact that this was the one and only time he had ventured above the parapet himself and joined his brave men, didn't seem to matter.

After a moment of inspiration (or was it madness?), which was mostly driven by consuming the whisky he hadn't shared with his men, he went over the top and immediately had his legs shot out from under him. The survivors said they heard him say, 'bloody Boche bad show.' and that he sobbed for his children, 'my beautiful girls' and 'time to pick up the mantle son.' The instruction that Guy still felt oppressed by and the girls delighted in.

It took about an hour or so for him to bleed to death, in the dark icy field with death shivering all around him. No one bothered to stretcher his cold prone body away, no one stayed with him, and it wouldn't have changed the outcome even if they had. It didn't distract from the fact that this was his most distinguished moment after a truly inglorious war.

Seventy-three men died with him, their shattered bloodied remains lying in a field somewhere for the most part forgotten. He was awarded a posthumous Victoria Cross for his bravery which mother gave to Guy. Guy rarely took it out of its box, he wanted no reminders of the war. He'd experienced the trenches himself and knew what that award meant, knew it might as well have been made of twisted bone, blood and fear. So, it lived in the kitchen drawer alongside the carving knife where it remained to this day.

Occasionally when it was quiet and they'd all gone to bed, he would open the drawer and he would watch it bleeding. 'There's blood here.' He would call out to the house and if someone came along, Guy would swear that he could hear the screams of men. Their youth, their future ebbing away with each painful and hard fought for breath. 'Make it stop.' 'Please stop.'

The house, which had recently learnt to Charleston, danced to Guy's tune and high-kicked the previous good order to the floor.

'Kick, snap and snake,' said an exhausted Mother from the yellow chinoiserie chaise longue that sat in the hall.

Guy had learnt that most men don't pass away quietly or indeed beautifully, as they do in art or novels; they die anguished and frustrated. If they are lucky they are in a hospital bed attached to a morphine drip confused and frightened. It isn't like a painting, you don't feel at peace, you are in an insanity of fear.

Knowing this was coming didn't make for an easy character.

He could be quite disturbed by the medal and would mutter to anyone that could hear, that he thought he could see the blood on his hands, smell the blood; that dreadful stench which would never leave his nostrils for as long as he lived.

It was normally Harriet that found him shaking in the corner, wringing his hands together, or at the sink scrubbing until his hands actually were really bleeding, which of course convinced him all the more. She'd been seeing this for some years now, so was used to the problem. And she didn't want to disturb Greta and wouldn't even contemplate letting the twins see him in this state.

Harriet had once seen Charity smirking at him, her pleasure caught, when he was having a 'difficult moment', so Harriet thought it best that she lead him to his chair and give him a top up of medicine. It seemed the only way to calm him. She grew up therefore with a love of special medicine, she took it herself sometimes and she had nice, extraordinary dreams or it gave her a little boost with her friends.

'A little soupcon never hurt anyone,' as Mother would say.

Harriet had never really known her father. George had reluctantly died when she was but a babe in arms. He'd left after just two days with his new daughter, so she could have had no memory of him, but she told everyone she knew him. Said she could remember his smell of whisky and pipe smoke.

Harriet missed him, missed the father figure. There was an absence which she tried to fill in many different

ways, none of them satisf.
she had found a bag of his
of which she had taken a fe
and one of his jumpers and b
she could and had even stole.
she wore most nights to keep
feel much closer to him.

Guy tried his best to nurture
moments of great tenderness for l
but he was too far gone to give   authority
figure and safety, that only an older .... can really give.

So, Harriet being Harriet had taken matters into her
own hands and had gone and found Nick, or had Nick
found her? She wasn't sure. Nick Jones, from the village
of Cubbington, who was no doubt awfully unsuitable, but
he smelt of alcohol and tobacco and that would do
Harriet for now.

Nick worked in the Cadena café in town and had first
seen Harriet, aged fifteen with Greta in tow. They had
ordered tea and pikelets with jam as well as butter. Harriet
was obviously excited at being in town and smiled wildly
at everyone, especially Nick, or so he thought.

Nick was forty one then. Two years later and he first
put his hand up her skirt. Harriet had screamed at first
and he'd put his hand over her mouth and so she bit and
struggled and cried. She didn't wash for days afterwards
because she liked the way her thighs smelt of tobacco, but
she understood this was a terrible problem and no one
would help her or believe her, or so she thought.

'Remember it's our little secret.'

Harriet despised him.

Since that moment she would often go to the cafe
when she was a bit bored just to torment Nick.
Unsolicited kicks would sometimes make him trip over.
Her satchel would be left at a difficult angle to upset his
path.

order everything on the menu and leave.

...on girls did not forgive and forget.

...ip it in the bud girls. Make them understand straight away it is not acceptable.' Mother's sage advice on such matters was firmly imprinted on her children.

It was night time in the park that made her happiest of course. She would meet Tustin, Hilary and Jack who were also escaping the difficulties of their home lives.

Tustin's mother had died recently of a massive heart attack; she hadn't been the same ever since her husband died on his trusty war horse, almost twenty years ago – an age. The horse miraculously returned (and wasn't turned into meat or glue like the majority of the others), but her husband never did make the journey home.

The now ancient horse was in a field on the Hilltop farm in Hunningham, a few miles away with the local lad, now farmer that had brought him back. Tustin said, he and his mother used to go and feed it apples. His mother used to ask the horse questions when they were there, questions about her husband. She always seemed satisfied with a nuzzle and thought the horse spoke back to her and they would have great long detailed conversations whilst a bored Tustin would roam the fields.

'It wasn't a surprise.' Tustin told his friends.

After her death, Tustin had become master of his house, wealthy beyond what he needed. But he was only a nineteen year old boy and had no idea whatever to do, or how he should behave. There didn't really seem to be much point to very much of anything.

He was part of an ever increasing misplaced generation of the original lost generation, who had one way or another, inadvertently in Tustin's case, absolutely in Guy's case been made old by the horrors of the war. His aunt was living with him and 'guiding' him, but she was so distraught she never knew whether she was coming or going. Just recently Tustin had spotted the laudanum bottle and saw her bus tickets to Hunningham and reckoned it was only a matter of time before he was alone again. He only hoped that she might manage to hold off until he was twenty-one so that the authorities would leave him alone. Only another two years - he thought it was possible.

Tustin had decided that his mission on becoming an orphan was to live the high life because who cared what might happen, the worst already had in his opinion. He was rich and could afford to forget in a manner to which he had grown unaccustomed to. He had roped his friends into his fun, why not! And the four of them enjoyed their new freedom and associated activities when they could and because they could.

'It is, it is, it is.'

If Guy had known about their shenanigans, he would have called them 'bright young things' as they were called in the papers when he was supposedly in his prime. But he felt that he had never really had a prime or felt bright, so it seemed a little odd.

Harriet was glad her siblings were unaware and imagined that her fun would stick in their throats somewhat.

'Fun! Fun Harriet, how incredibly infantile,' said Grace on more than one occasion.

'You are not five,' smirked Charity.

But Mother winked from the portrait in the hall. Mother understood pleasure.

It was a little more difficult for Hilary and Jack as they had parents and importantly carers, with everything that word means, that were compos-mentis enough to wonder where they were.

Still, they all managed to meet under the clock tower most Tuesday and Thursday evenings. Harriet and Tustin had become quite friendly after their last meeting. They had dared one another to shimmy up the bright blue painted wrought iron bridge and dangle over the weir, hold it for as long as they could before shimmying back down again. Harriet found this hilarious and currently held the highest and fastest score.

'Not bad for a bloody girl Harry.'

She was quite a tomboy and had always been quick, whether it was climbing trees, climbing over gates or shimmying up bridges. To date none of them had crashed into the weir and the white water below.

At other times they took it in turns to offer up a bare leg and hold it very still, whilst the white powder was dusted out of Tustin's silver pot, which they had christened Pandora's Box. Whether or not this box contained all the evils of the world was yet to be determined but it seemed appropriate that in the story of Pandora when she opened the lid and everything bad escaped, hope was left inside. That's how it felt to Tustin, surrounded by madness but hope was somewhere safely locked up. It wasn't entirely out of reach.

'There is always hope.'

'The most precious commodity.'

He also explained to the others that just like Pandora once they had lifted the lid and done this terrible thing, it could never be undone. But unlike his mythical counterpart, neither Tustin nor the others regretted a moment because they were having far too much fun. Pandora's Box would be shaken gently and a whole pound note was rolled up ready to use. This in itself was incredibly indulgent and the arrogance of that act used to excite Harriet almost beyond any effect of the actual powder.

'Fuck forever.'

They would take it in turns to inhale. Harriet and Hillary used to try and get each other's legs as they were smoother and the powder didn't get caught up with the hairier men's legs. Although Harriet had to admit to

Hilary that recently it was quite exciting for Tustin to offer up his naked leg. They all used to sit quite closely for ten minutes for the special treat to take effect. Then they would dance, shimmy up bridges, sing and play in the dark night time locked park, that often smelt of honeysuckle and that peculiar smell of the river. Intoxication.

It was a childhood of sorts that they felt they had most definitely lost, in fact, in the case of Harriet and Tustin, weren't even sure they had to begin with. They could lose themselves for hours. The other night they had ended up running through the fountains fully dressed. They were left on for some reason, they weren't sure why, but they were utterly delighted and utterly soaking. The ducks just watched them, they'd seen it all before, but the swans weren't very happy and Jack had been bitten which had only just about healed up now. They rubbed some of the magic powder into it. He wasn't sure if it had any effect on his injury but it did mean he didn't care less.

The following day Harriet was walking through the park with Greta, who thought she looked peaky and needed some fresh air. Harriet could have sworn that the swans remembered her, squawking and screaming as they went close by the water.

Greta wondered if even the swans could tell she was a German.

'Let's go home shall we?'

CHAPTER 6

It was a wet Wednesday afternoon, the rain had begun to pitter and patter on the windows, echoing on the old glass greenhouse with the birdcage roof. Harriet pottered around, popping in the seeds that Tustin had given her into a fresh patch of earth. She wondered if anything would happen, but it was worth a go and besides her sisters rarely ventured into the greenhouse in the day time.

'Pollen dear, pollen. It can creep upon one even in the coldest of autumns, there is contamination everywhere. Vigilance is key!' Explained Charity.

'We are delicate creatures dear, we cannot sneeze or trouble our bronchial pipes,' stated Grace.

'Delicate, my arse,' muttered Harriet.

And three dazzling smiles ended the conversation.

Very occasionally, Guy would absentmindedly wander around in a daze, picking of dead heads here and there. Harriet had once seen him drag in the gramophone, pop on his straw boater and dance and talk to the flowers as if they were his friends.

'Boom boom de boom' he sang as he danced a bossa nova around the dahlias.

The dahlias shrank away in surprise, but the petunias positively triumphed and a growth spurt ensued. A magpie smashed into the glass and a little chip appeared in the window.

But it was rare any of them were in there, so Harriet thought it was worth a go. She didn't think they'd know what they were anyway and wasn't even sure if she'd recognise it if it did grow. Worried that she might think any growth were weeds, she left a little pebble next to each spot, so she wouldn't forget where they were.

Once her gardening task was complete she went into Greta in the kitchen and asked if they could go to the Cadena cafe.

'It will be my treat Greta, Guy has just given me my allowance and besides I think we need cheering up after the swans were so fierce this morning, what do you think?'

She grinned, even suggesting that she may need cheering up was a sure-fire way of getting Greta to accompany her. She felt the need to torment undeserving fools.

'I would be honoured to accompany such a lovely young lady.'

Greta smiled indulgently and pinched the cheek of little thoughtful Harriet and went to reach for her coat, but just at that moment the twins came in and said they would be having a visitor to tea, in the shape of Uncle William, so could Greta please rustle up some little rolls and a Victoria sponge.

'Pleased to see you here too dear, where have you been? Your fingernails are all grubby, run along upstairs and take a bath would you, he'll be here within a few hours and we need to make Mummy proud, don't we?'

'Mummy is dead Grace, I'm quite sure she doesn't care whether I have dirty fingernails or not and besides the water will be cold.'

'The cold will be good for your soul Harriet. Whatever do you mean, of course Mummy is here, she is always here, you know better than that, now run along.'

Harriet and Greta exchanged glances and Harriet slumped off upstairs, how they infuriated her.

'Greta, please use the duck egg plates, the breakfast set, I think they are about the best.'

Grace smiled, she remembered the day Greta's husband died too.

Greta's heart sank as it always did at the thought of the china ware, but she got the plates ready anyway.

Uncle William, Mother's brother, generally despaired over his sister's children and made sure he lived at the other end of the country. Scotland to be exact, so as he didn't have to see them very often. Childless himself by choice, he struggled rather with the role his careless sister had left him.

'Bloody Hermione Lucretia Codrington,' he would mutter.

'Incredibly and unbearably careless and selfish to die before sixty when one has young children. Get them over the age of consent at least.' He would tell anyone that would listen.

It was William who had assured the solicitors that Guy was more than capable of looking after his sisters now that they were orphaned, anything to save himself the hideous task. He couldn't care less if that were true, he had come back from the war alive, hadn't he? All limbs and heart intact, what more could they want? He got that German woman in to help, what more did they need?

'Self-sufficiency is a wonderful virtue, isn't it? And I'm such an encouragement.'

He told himself he needed the country air of Scotland, his dogs, his guns and his whisky. He liked to combine all three quite often. A stiff drink and a bit squiffy, then on with the wax jacket, grab a dog and shoot things. He found it calming and pleasurable. Made up for the fact that he didn't go to the Front, didn't go anywhere in fact on account of him shooting himself in the foot and presenting a terrible limp at the time. Managed to persuade them it was a shooting accident, chasing after a poacher.

'The scourge of the countryside – stealing good meat that could go to the troops.'

And so, he had been assigned the job of Countryside Supply Manager, which didn't really alter his life one jolt, just meant more people went with him to shoot at things, but they didn't get their hands on his whisky. And little had changed in that respect now.

Occasionally he would hear comments or notice disapproving looks when he ventured into the village or nearest town, even now with the whispers of another war beginning.

'Didn't feel quite up to the war.'

'How he lives with himself I don't know.'

This just made him go home and shoot more things. If he could terrify a rabbit or a badger, it made him feel like the other men, mindlessly shooting things. He took out his aggression and it restored his sense of manliness.

Sometimes after too much whisky he would weep and bury some of the sorry creatures and say prayers. And when he awoke in the morning with a headache and feeling out of sorts he would have a hair of the dog and after lunch, possibly a Bordeaux and the cycle would begin all over again.

When he ever thought of his family, he managed to tell himself that the children were grown-ups now. Well Harriet would be shortly, and he would be so relieved as soon as she turned twenty-one, but he would feel a little better when she turned twenty-five.

'Well that will be that.'

His weary watchful eyes would never have to go to Leamington Spa again and all its ridiculous gentrification, wouldn't have to take that disgusting water, walk in those self- conscious, prettified gardens, walk the length of the Parade, smiling at people he didn't care for. No, he wouldn't have to leave the countryside of Dumfries and Galloway again. He could stay in his big stone solid house in Haugh of Urr and shut the world away. He couldn't wait!

The twins however, adored Uncle William. After all, he was a small part of their mother and they looked for her in everything he said or did.

'Was Mother terribly beautiful as a child, Uncle?'

'Did Mother have many proposals, Uncle?'

'I expect she was awfully kind, wasn't she?'

'Do you think we are like her, Uncle?'

And so, the questions continued, which he found exhausting. He had learnt to not really say much other than yes, as there was something about those girls that made him want to keep them happy and in love with him. Hadn't fathomed why, other than he thought they were a little bit like his sister and in that respect, he was a little afraid of them.

Greta went to find Guy and found him in an agitated state at the prospect of Uncle William visiting. He was pacing in the drawing room and he had a damp forehead, which he was frantically dabbing at with a handkerchief.

Greta felt for this young man, made old. Thirty-seven now with the responsibility of a family and this house thrust upon him. Doing his duty and returning from France to look after the girls as best he could after his mother had died. Guy hoped he wouldn't want to see any household accounts, God knew where they were. All Guy ever worried about was whether there were any creditors and at this time there were not, which should satisfy his uncle.

Guy hadn't yet realised that when his uncle, locked himself in his room, to give the books a thorough going over, he in fact gave a very short, perfunctory to say the least, glance and then had a snooze, anything to bide himself some time away from them. There was no other way that Guy would be patted on the back each visit.

'Keep up the good work old boy.'

In fact, if Uncle did ever spot anything, which he quite often did, he ignored it. The last thing he wanted was the girls to have to live with him or something equally dreadful.

The family had given up paying Greta much other than pocket money, which had saved them some funds and she didn't ask for a proper wage because she lived with them for free, it didn't seem correct. Besides she knew that Guy couldn't really afford it and she was terrified that if she asked, he might say he had to let her go and then where on earth would she go. Not back to Germany, which was impossible.

'Greta, splendid Greta, where would we be without you?' I suppose we should decant the port for our visitor and I should just check it is ok, so if you wouldn't mind Greta and bring it into my study that would be most kind.'

Greta smiled and turned away, she made a mental note to check on him in half an hour's time, or else that may be the last any of them saw of him for the rest of the day. She prepared the drink and then returned to the kitchen to make the sponge. It would use up their last egg, but it was a special occasion of sorts.

As she went in search of the flour, she found a dripping wet Harriet in the pantry, pools of water following her progress. She had her mouth around the cooking sherry, Greta really must remember to lock it up or else come Christmas time there would be none left. Disturbed, she spilt her last sip down her chin and it fell down onto her chest. How she wished it was a park night and Tustin could take advantage of it. Oh well, she'd best get dressed for Uncle William instead,

'Oops sorry Greta, how deadly of me.'

And with that she sloped off upstairs with a lopsided grin on her face.

CHAPTER 7

Grace and Charity retreated to their rooms, in order to prepare themselves for their relation. Grace chose the almost iridescent pink dress of their mothers and let Charity wear the white this time. They took it in turns, the white being both their favourites. They shared a dab or two of Mother's perfume, thankfully they had been sparing in their usage and there was still almost a third of a bottle left. Heavens knew what they would do when it ran dry. Not as if Guy would be returning to France anytime soon and they simply couldn't leave the house for a trip away, not as things were. They had a terrible responsibility.

'The white is magnificent dear, it's like looking in a mirror.'

'And the pink brings out the delicate glow to your cheeks darling.'

The twins were undoubtedly stunning, almost angelic in their appearance. Their long white hair fell about their shoulders. In the half light of an autumn evening, it almost looked Godly, like a halo, glowing for the old house to see.

Even the damp walls paused in deference.

They also seemed to glide somewhat around the house and their footsteps were as quiet as little church mice.

'Shhhhh now treasures, revel in the surprise,' instructed Mother.

Quite often, Harriet found herself unknowingly in the company of one or both of her sisters. It could be a little unnerving. Mostly, they went together everywhere of course. It was very rare to find one of them alone, or at least not within a few meters of one another. They hardly ever ventured outside. Instead Greta was sent out, if there were any dealings to be had with 'the public' or 'people that do'. Jobs such as the post office, shopping and the like, was most definitely down to Greta and occasionally Harriet's domain. When they did go out they were something akin to local celebrities. People whispered as their swan necks glided past them; there was always chatter about the strange yet beautiful Leighton sisters.

'So elegant, correct and upstanding, so unlike that younger wilder sister of theirs, who could be so uncouth.' No doubt 'these were ladies, old fashioned in a very good way, not at all like the rest of the youth of today.'

The twins were spoken of in hushed tones and looked upon with awe. How could people so beautiful have a bad bone in their body?

They went to 'dreadful occasions' a few times a year and were always photographed. The flashlight and their general whiteness jumping of the page was like a lightning bolt and everyone beheld them, you simply couldn't take your eyes off them. How they hated these events, it made them feel quite nauseous. So, they very rarely spoke or ate much but felt that the good name of the Leighton's must be upheld, and it would not do to be totally reclusive as poor dear Guy could simply not be relied upon.

'We must be brave darling and do as Mother would.'

They did their duty and carried themselves in such a way as they hoped would make their mother proud. Mother after all loved a good party, this was well known to everyone. The twins expected she was only doing her duty and simply doing it very well and was very much admired. They didn't realise the exciting and much sought-after liaisons and the secrets and the drinks that their dear mother so enjoyed.

'It's our little secret.'

'Be bold and quick.'

'J'adore.'

Inside the big old white house with the green door they tried in vain to separate themselves from their siblings as best they could. They occupied the front rooms, with the most light shining in. It was very good for the skin, or so they had heard, and they were also fans of moon bathing, just as their mother had taught them. It was knowledge that was fed through the generations of Codrington women. 'The purest form of light.' 'A celestial body transforming our souls.' 'The very essence of femininity.'

This revolutionary technique involved opening the curtains at night and letting the moonlight flood in. It was best to be naked apparently, but the girls covered up with a simple silk shift and exposed little parts of themselves bit by bit, never fully exposed at once. It was best to be safe as they didn't want to lead any passers-by into temptations. There were standards. They were aware that they were considered beauties.

'What can one do?' 'One cannot escape, one's genes.'

'We are prisoners to these outward shells.'

The girls felt it was stupefying and wonderful to be basking under the cooling luminous rays of the moon, bringing the very core of their femaleness to the fore. They felt energised and refreshed. Mother said that their grandmother used to practice outside, the cool night air adding to the effects of the bathe.

Once or twice a year, the girls followed in Granny's footsteps and did the same, although Grace, it had to be said mostly liked to bathe indoors. Charity however, loved the way the cool air hardened her nipples and the way the wind brushed against her body. It added a certain zing.

'How one trembles.'

'Ting-a-ling-ling, bathing on the wing.'

As it was the practice to massage oneself as one bathed, she enjoyed squeezing and vigorously rubbing her body when she was outside.

'Stimulate the blood, get those ions fizzing, girls.'

Once Grace had retired, she felt compelled to touch herself between her legs, which was one of the very few secrets she kept from her sister. She had discovered the process was best enjoyed in a light drizzle, as the droplets awakened her no end. Charity felt she should enter into the event fully, which she did when she could.

'No half measures, not for my girls,' said Mother from her portrait by the stairs.

Although Grace followed the correct procedure of massaging one's upper torso, she was far more pragmatic than her sister and felt she should just do the necessary and retire to bed as soon after her practice, so as not to catch a chill. This was a medicinal procedure and not for enjoyment after all.

In fact, it was on Grace's insistence that they only practised this more extreme moon bathe once or twice a year, as she had suspicions that her sister was enjoying the practice too much, and it was for health not pleasure. The two could not co-exist happily.

Other gentler times indoors were recommended as much as possible, for cooling and stilling the mind. However, the full moon bathe was particularly important and so very good for the artists that they were. As such, they had quite a routine on a full moon day and kept a calendar that charted the phases of the moon, with each full moon day blacked out as they had a very busy schedule and it would be too terrible to miss it.

In the evening they would have a mineral salt bath, the

water aligning with the moon, the minerals sent into a healthy healing overdrive. All those little ions just fizzing away! Grace had read it created a magnetic field, which she liked the sound of as it sounded powerful.

Once the bath was over, it was important to let the body dry naturally. They did this by eleven star jumps each, then they pulled open the curtains to their room and let the moon fill every pore. They could spend hours this way and it made them feel wonderful and Harriet suspected even paler and if possible more beautiful the next day.

Grace's room had once been their mother's bedroom and Charity occupied her old sitting room. They had of course kept most of her belongings and could be heard by Greta and Harriet to talk to her often. The rooms were painted a pale shade of yellow to maximise the light and they had made Guy and Greta paint the furniture white. They had checked it once with Mummy and they were sure that she didn't mind, so bit by bit every bit of furniture had been 'paled'. The rooms were at odds with the rest of the house, with its heavy mahogany and faded grandeur. Their rooms positively sparkled in comparison.

'It needs to sparkle.'

'…and dazzle.'

The house was terrified into submission in these rooms and there was little damp here.

Their other space in the house was the old attic room, once the nursery now their art room, as it had become. Very different from their rooms downstairs, the attic was dark with special lighting rigged up for working in the night time which they did often and yet occasionally they would stick to good old-fashioned candlelight, if they seemed to think their paintings needed a little more atmosphere. It was also at the front of the house and far enough away from Greta's little room for it to cause them any inconvenience or annoyance.

The girls had always painted, encouraged by both their parents who indulged them terribly. Their father had luckily died before he could see them continue and develop as artists. As this was not something that his girls should ever consider.

'Hobbies are fine, but they must concentrate their lessons on becoming good wives.'

It was fine as children, but as adults, no. The girls should be considering marriage and not tiring themselves unnecessarily. Conversely, Mother actively encouraged it. She had insisted that they paint her often and there were reminders on every space of wall available.

'I really think this look should be captured for posterity.'

Mother's favourite painting of herself hung downstairs in the drawing room for all to admire, at her insistence of course, but Greta would forever be finding little sketches and cartoons all over the house as the girls had left them overtime.

They were up in the attic often, every day for some time at least. Late at night, Guy sometimes thought he heard them in there, although his thinking was becoming increasingly foggy and he could easily be mistaken. The girls had a new series of drawings on the go at the moment that seemed to be the view from the hallway just behind the attic. It looked out onto the back garden, onto specifically the greenhouse roof, dozens of sketches of the birdcage ceiling everywhere.

Charity had even begun to sketch the visiting birds in the garden, which drank and washed in the bird bath she'd repositioned, so she could view it from her room. Occasionally she even ventured out into the garden to draw her new obsession, capturing each feather, each claw, and each eye in incredible detail. She was especially delighted if Milly the cat had killed a bird. She found the remains fascinating and she loved the way a drop of crimson added a new dimension to the drawing.

'Inspection and keen observation will serve you well my girls,' said Mother.

Grace preferred the birdcage roof itself, although even she was not immune to sketching a little bird or two into her drawings, her favourite being the magpie. There was something about the noise it made when it had just caught a mouse or some other little creature. She liked their tenacity and boldness, they seemed to be absolutely unafraid of her, which she admired. She found it oddly soothing.

'Be bold, be brave, and be eager,' as Mother was fond of telling them.

CHAPTER 8

Greta went to check on Guy and found him dozing in the window, an empty port glass in his hand and it looked like rather more than one glass had been consumed. She had not been quick enough this time. Damn that Victoria sponge.

Waking him gently, she led him upstairs to his room, thinking that a little sleep in his bed would steady him until the arrival. It would do him no good, if she were to wake him suddenly and ask him to get ready. Yes, a little sleep was best for all concerned. And if their uncle arrived early, she would make a little excuse to bide him some time. In any case the twins would be the stars of the show, keen to spend every moment with their uncle, who looked so much like their mother.

Both were small fair people, prone to more than a little plumpness, although this didn't seem to be especially genetic as none of the children were. Their mother was plump, as once their father had died, she took not quite entirely to her bed, but spent most of the reminder of her days in the house, and a large proportion of that time was spent lounging in her rooms eating bonbons.

'I must conserve, what little energy I have.'

Very occasionally she would make the young twins push her in her bath chair outdoors, but this was only on rare occasions, when the situation absolutely demanded it.

'I'm grieving, I'm too exhausted.'

'Together, you have the strength of a lion.'

It was Harriet that suffered the most with this feverish inertia.

Her father died and left her as an infant with her mother for her remaining fifteen years or so. For the most part, Mother had lost a lot of interest and rarely played or spoke with her youngest child. The only real moments of tenderness came at night time when Harriet was invited to her rooms to chat and occasionally to sleep.

'Come and lie with me little one.'

For the most part, Greta took on the role of mothering teenage Harriet, after Mother had finally succumbed. Guy, much older than his little sister, did his bit when and where he could but again it wasn't his forte and there had been the 'accident', which troubled Greta.

For most of Harriet's childhood, he had been in France, but when he returned, he remembered his baby sister fondly and their bond returned too. A natural, unbreakable tie. In fact, she had been his only reason for returning. She offered him the opportunity of trying again.

Uncle William's plumpness came from gluttony and sadness which led him to overeat and drink. He had lost his sister, not that they had been particularly close, but still he adored her and having no family of his own, he felt the loss and felt the last of the line.

Her children may still be going strong, but he doubted if any of them would ever produce a child to carry on the gene pool.

'Bloody disrespectful.'

Guy was a lost cause, especially after the loss of that French child. The twins absolutely not, they seemed to have no real interest in men at all and as for Harriet, well as for Harriet, maybe there was still time for her to sort herself out, time would tell.

Bemused by this unfathomable interest in their procreation, the Leighton girls gave this topic the short shrift it rightly deserved.

'We are unique Uncle. And that is that.'

'A pale imitation would not suffice, surely that is rather obvious.'

And Harriet called him a 'condescending dinosaur' which she rather hoped he would overhear.

And Guy remembered Unity and struggled to hold back a tear.

No-one enjoyed this particular topic.

All the same, Harriet dressed for her dear uncle, whom she couldn't give two hoots about. She hated how he seemed to cross examine Guy, hated how her sisters sucked up to him at any given opportunity.

In a bold move, she decided to go for father's waistcoat with a pair of trousers she had recently made out of some black material Hilary had given her. She added a touch of kohl to her eyes and sat on her bed, determined not to emerge until she had heard the doorbell, so that there was no chance for any of them to force her to change into a sweet little tea dress.

Downstairs Greta had completed her preparations, the guest room had been made up, and she had lit a fire in the grate in case he wanted to retire after his journey. The cake and rolls were baking nicely, and the tea service set out with the pretty lace table cloth. The port had been replenished and the stopper pushed very firmly in. She had even been outside and picked some mixed evergreens for the table. Peeling off her apron and fishing a comb out of her pocket to run quickly through her hair finished the preparations. Greta was ready and had done all of this, in the time it took the others to fall apart, dress and fall apart again.

She took to her chair in the kitchen and waited.

The house quickly weaved a trail when no-one was looking.

CHAPTER 9

He was over an hour late when he finally arrived, tired and aggrieved by the taxi driver who had met him from the station.

'A ridiculous expense for a trip of less than a mile, these new motor cars are a terrible invention. Didn't use to have any of this trouble with the old horse and cab and they call this progress.' Uncle William was of an age when everything that was over thirty years old was new.

Charity met him and insisted that he rest for a while after his hardships.

'How terrible Uncle, I suggest a little rest before tea, how does that sound?' And Charity kissed him on the cheek and led an indulged and relieved William upstairs.

After she had settled him, she went into Grace and they decided to brush each other's hair again until it absolutely shone like the sun.

Greta's Victoria sponge had little sweet iced diamonds on the top in yellow and green, which secretly Harriet adored, not that she would let that show of course. Instead she picked at her food, swirling it around her plate whilst intermittently sighing and glowering at Uncle William.

Tip tap tippity toe, the clock ticked and Guy's

fingernails were picked.

'God this is boring', thought Harriet and she suspected Uncle William didn't really want to be there either.

Uncle William meanwhile was lost somewhere in the woods in his borderlands and nodding when he felt it appropriate.

Harriet knew that dutiful look and that one thought made her admire him a little bit, who would want to be here after all?

'Oops silly me, I've dropped my cake on the floor.'

Harriet desperate to make something of interest happen, was pleased to see Charity scowl.

'What ho Guy.'

Guy had emerged for tea and luckily their uncle was oblivious to his little 'nap'.

'Hello my boy, you look well.'

'Thank you yes, Uncle William, very well indeed.'

Guy seemed on form, much to the twin's annoyance. It was almost as if they wanted Uncle to find their brother drunk and/or incompetent. Yet, instead he found a picture of a happy beautiful family. The girls were unusually charming, Harriet even heard Grace giggle - an odd wattle wattle sound which was unheard of and quite extraordinary. The strange gaggling noise even seemed to surprise Charity somewhat, who jolted in her chair at the sound.

William couldn't help but look in wonder at the twins. Remarkable how these beautiful sparkling bright young women were related to him. They were luminescent in every way and their pale dresses made them look so terribly angelic. Such a shame they were rather peculiar he mused; they could be a perfect charm on his arm, or on any man's.

'Any social events girls?'

'Only when we have to Uncle, we do our duty you know.'

'Of course dear, any special friends I should be aware of?' William asked hopefully, already knowing the answer.

'Dear Uncle, we only attend functions for duties sake, how frivolous we would be to consider friends.'

'When would we have the time? We are married to our art dear Uncle.'

'Friends are for those who lack the standing we do or have little ability. The sociable are so pedestrian, don't you agree?'

Harriet smirked.

'Harriet, we have each other' and Harriet received a very tight squeeze to the arm.

Satisfied, well in truth, utterly relieved that all seemed to be well, Uncle William thought he should retire for the rest of the evening. Thank heavens, he wouldn't have to step in. Despite Charity's letter, seeming to profess all was not well and that maybe he should come and stay and see what he thought, all seemed fine. The poor girl was obviously a little tired on the day she wrote, Guy seemed to be managing three women better than he ever could!

Uncle William had never understood a Codrington woman.

Uncle William didn't understand Leighton women either.

The twins, of course were a little disappointed, they were looking forward to showing him their latest collection of pictures of Mummy that afternoon. They had even had one framed to take away with him. Still, it would wait until breakfast and he knew best, all the Codrington's did.

Uncle William sighed at his sister on the wall.

'Nighty night dear Chubbs,' she replied.

The twins retired to the attic after tea and continued with their bird and conservatory pictures. Grace was concentrating on the wings more than anything, which was her latest thing. Harriet faced with another evening watching Guy lost in his thoughts, flounced to the bookshelves to find something to take away some of her boredom, and Greta went to the kitchen to clear up. She banked on them not needing an evening meal as tea had been so late. Guy patrolled the house and garden, smoking a cigarette as he went.

'Clunk, click, check and pull.'

He obsessively checked three times that all the doors were locked, checked and then double checked. He then made the rounds of each room, turning of lights as he went. Upstairs there was the smell of violets again and he shuddered. He heard what sounded like sobbing and he caught the eye of one of Mother's portraits, at which he nodded and carried on his way.

'Leave me be Mother.'

He finally ended up in the small drawing room with a glass of sherry and the clocks ticked, the lights flickered, the wax dripped and the walls bled, just like every other evening. Harriet joined him a while afterwards, book in hand and positioned herself under the light by the window. A chink in the curtains let her gaze out onto the street. She saw lovers' arm in arm go by, cabs pull off, laughter, a group of men went into the pub, and a dog ran by. She glimpsed life when inside there was none, well none that made any sense to her.

'Would you like to go out for once Guy?' We could take a late walk?'

Guy watched his sister looking out at the world and felt that they were much safer here inside, away from all the madness. He could understand that she was young and hated being cooped up inside with the rest of the family. But she should understand that it was dangerous out there and he didn't want to let what happened to Unity to happen to her. He didn't think he could continue if that happened. This was the second chance and it was important. If only he could just focus.

'It's getting cold Harry, best stay warm and dry.'

Unity was a sweet and pretty child and they were living on the Ile d'Oleron at the time that the terrible thing happened. It was a magical place only accessible by boat, cut off from the mainland, which was how they liked it. The fort was no longer occupied, as it had been in the war and they felt life and hope returning to them. They had been there for two years and had gone there to Cheri's home town, after the war had ended. They had to leave the coast and the north, where Guy had done his stint in the trenches. Understandably that was non-negotiable.

They needed an escape plan and it was unthinkable to return to England, especially after his father had died in the trenches.

'There are ghosts there Cheri.'

Guy knew he would be reminded of the war at every turn if he returned, and he wasn't inclined to indulge in the fantasy that was his father. No, it was safer to stay in France. Safer than that house.

'And, she is all encompassing. Mother demands the untenable.'

His French was improving and Cheri was radiant, Unity their first child an absolute joy. It was almost as if the horrors of war hadn't happened. Guy supposed she had been too young to remember any of them. She was a free and happy child and liked the rockier beaches on the north east of the island best, as she loved digging around in the rock pools with Guy. They could spend hours out there, looking for crabs and other creatures.

And very soon this child became all-encompassing to Guy too.

Carrying a little bucket and a giggle that was ever ready to use when she caught one of 'the little monsters' Unity was as enthralled with her father. Cheri would watch from a sunny point on the rocks, smiling at her new-found contentment.

They ate mussels and oysters and sprinkled them with the islands salt. They went to the market at St Pierre. Guy played boules in the square and they would sit in cafes with their café au lait and Unity would have freshly squeezed fruit juice. It was a tonic. Few on the island spoke of their shared recent history, there was no need to remember.

Life was brand new again.

Occasionally, about once a fortnight they would catch the little ferry to the mainland and go to La Rochelle, but they were always so keen to return to their island home. Guy would visit the post office in the main town sending and receiving telegrams from Leamington Spa, the town he didn't want to return to. Guy heard about his little sister. Just a little child, not much older than Unity in years; in fact, he could see a small resemblance.

'You have abandoned me to my fate.' Mother would write.

And his teenage sisters would write in great detail about 'Mother's great sadness' and draw him pictures of her.

'Mother is an angel.'

'Mother is so brave.'

Guy missed the thought of Harriet, but only her. It became important that he write to her despite her not being able to understand. Could she even read yet? He liked to think that the twins or mother, would tell her about him.

'Another holiday note from my distant son,' Mother would wail. To Mother, Guy was on an extended and terribly selfish holiday. He was not French. What was he thinking?

'Ridiculous darlings, stay with Mummy always.' And the twins would kiss dear Mamma and swear that they would absolutely.

Guy's letters were given to the twins for their creations.

'Create Mummy something beautiful from this cruel distant boy's words.'

When Guy left, his twin sisters were just little girls.

'Young ladies from a Royal spa town,' I think you'll find.

Even then, they were resourceful and only really had a need for each other. Their beauty was enough to make Father proud and Mother did enjoy schooling her girls.

'Silly Guy, we don't need you.' They would tell him and even when they were children, this was unquestionably correct.

'Codrington girls are self-sufficient, they'll be no pandering to the male ego.' Mother was quite sure about it.

Mother was spiralling into blackness after his father had died and he couldn't tolerate her and that. All of that.

Some would have said he should have returned and been the man of the family.

'I require a man.' Mother was quite plain about it. But he felt life was so short and precious that he intended to be as happy as he could be; and that meant France, it meant his wife and child. It meant the sun on his face.

Guy saw his beautiful wife laughing and swimming in the sea, waving and calling out to him. They often swam naked together, and he felt her body rub against his, felt her small waist and the curve of her thigh.

Felt it, in a cold room in the big white house with the green front door.

The last time he touched a woman, he couldn't bring himself to look at her in the face – it wasn't the body he knew every lump, bump and curve of. He'd tried a few times since, but each time he saw her walking out of the sea, the water dripping from her breasts, felt her lying next to him and it was all too much. The medicine took away the sting.

In the chilly room in 1935, those years felt a million miles away, was he really that happy ten, fifteen years ago.

'How it speeds up this life, it was so long ago now.'

'And yet at night, it is yesterday.'

He had been a young vital man then, and now as he approached middle age he felt the years. He drifted back and felt the sun again, heard the waves lapping onto the beach, the rhythmic lapping over and over again, tasted the salt on his lips, felt his child's hand grip his. The tears came.

'Goodnight Guy.'

'Au revoir mon petite.'

Harriet did her duty and left him as she always did. He would come to in a few hours and he would either take himself on a tour of the house before bed or Greta would come and gently guide him to his room. It was only very occasionally that he stayed there and sometimes Harriet would drift off and spend the night there with him. Not tonight however, she was quite tired after Uncle William's visit and for once fancied a quiet night herself.

She took herself into the kitchen and warmed up some milk in a pan. One of the twins had left one of their bird pictures on the side. The bird was dead and its neck twisted, blood had been painted on its feathers and in a pool around its poor little body. Horrible.

'Examine.'

Harriet wondered about her sisters at times, she really did. She expected it was quite harmless and they'd spied it like that in the morning. Maybe Milly the cat had been having adventures the night before and this was the result.

Either way, she popped it in the drawer, the one that contained all the other pictures she and the others had found left strewn around. There was quite a selection of mutilated birds, bird's eyes, bird's wings, really rather grisly. She found a few of her mother and she felt sad.

'It is what it is,' she heard Guy mumble.

The woman she hadn't really known, who seemed to have just gone to sleep that night in May and never woken up. Harriet missed her and sighed. There were only scant memories of the night she died, but the one she did remember was holding her mother's hand, their fingers entwined. Harriet wasn't sure if she was dead or alive at that point, but she remembered thinking how white her hands were as the moon bathed the room in all its lustrous glory.

The milk boiled over, 'damn'. She fetched her mother's china cup, the one she had with her that night. It was very pretty with little pink rosebuds and blue cornflowers. It had over time acquired a little chip in the corner, but tonight it was the only one that would do. She poured what remained of the liquid and took the drink upstairs to bed with her. It was quiet as she went up the mahogany wooden flight.

'Up the wooden stairs to Bedfordshire darling.'

She heard her mother's voice and counted quietly as she used to when she was little, her voice with its playful lilt.

'One, two buckle my shoe, three, four open the door, five six fiddle sticks.'

She reached the point where she could clearly see her mother's picture which seemed to watch her moving up the staircase tonight and spoke softly.

'I miss you.'

'Everything is all right now.'

She heard her mother's voice echo in her head and she smelt the same violet smell that Guy had done earlier that evening. The house seemed to bathe in violets today.

Somewhere a window banged shut and Harriet ran the rest of the way to her room, the tears dripping into her milk which made it taste a little salty. It wasn't unpleasant.

CHAPTER 10

The next morning at the breakfast table, with those duck egg blue plates, the family sat together as was the norm and ate. What was far from the norm was how chatty and animated the twins were, positively motherly to Harriet. They declared that they rather fancied taking the air that morning, which really was quite surprising to the others. Harriet suspected it was a ruse for Uncle William's benefit, to show him how caring they were and how Harriet was in safe hands.

'Harriet darling you really must try and eat more you know, we worry about you we really do.'

'Yes, do come along dear and do as your sisters ask, no one likes a skinny minny, you know, certainly not in these parts.'

'Uncle's right Harriet, it may be all the rage in London, but it isn't here, so do please eat more.'

'Here we go again,' sighed Harriet inwardly.

And the ceiling created a rather beautiful floral shape in its manoeuvrings.

Harriet choked the food down just to shut them up and Greta gave her a wink. The little one had red eyes this morning and Greta knew she'd been sobbing over something.

After breakfast Guy and Uncle William retired to the

front room to discuss 'business' whatever that meant. Harriet had no idea and didn't care. But she was pleased it meant Uncle William wouldn't be lingering around getting in her way, worse still expecting her to indulge in any sort of activity.

She offered to walk with Greta into the town and help with her jobs, anything to get away from the house. She ran up the stairs to grab her coat, giving a cursory glance towards her mother in the frame. The face seemed quite benign this morning and still. Harriet imagined a faint smile at the corner of the mouth and it made her feel better.

'Goodbye Mother.'

'Goodbye darling.'

At the door she was amazed to see her sisters waiting with Greta. They really were going out and it seemed they had their notepad and crayons with them, which was a relief as it meant they didn't intend to 'take the air' with them at least.

Stranger still, Harriet was kissed on the cheek which felt icy cold on her skin, but she took it in the way she hoped it was offered and smiled at them both.

'Wrap up well darling and Greta don't let her get cold now will you.'

'Of course not Miss Leighton, we'll be all right won't we Harriet?'

Autumn had quickly turned to winter and it was a beautiful wonderland day outside. Crisp and bright, the sunlight dancing around the white buildings, the frost dancing in the trees. Leamington could truly be beautiful thought Greta, maybe not on a par with Germany and the wonderful glistening forests, but for today at least she was happy to be where she was.

Soon they were on the Parade and at the post office building on the corner of Leam Terrace, before making their way up the street, over the bridge and stopping at

Dunns department store for some essentials. The rest was normally delivered, but a few things were still needed immediately. After they had done their jobs Harriet persuaded Greta to go to the Cadena, for a hot drink.

'Well the twins seemed to be so concerned that we should catch cold, I really think we should stop, before we reach home.'

And Greta was a little tired so indulged her and very soon cocoa and hot buttered toast with a side order of angry flirting was being served. As Greta went to pay the bill, Nick came to clear the plates, dropped a knife under Harriet's chair and took the opportunity to place his hand on her legs.

Harriet giggled a strange wattle wattle, surprisingly like her sister. A little like a goose she thought. A worrying sound. You do not mess with a goose.

She rocked ever so slightly to give him a little illicit thrill and then to give herself a reciprocal little thrill she picked up the knife and dug it as hard as she could into the side of his leg.

'What a pretty smile you have dear heart,' said an unknowing Greta from afar. She felt rather pleased with herself that the cocoa had nourished her so much so, she could see the colour rise in young Harriet's cheeks. Yes, she was a good guardian.

Nick had gasped with a peculiar strangulated silent scream and at that moment she herself felt an enormous amount of pleasure, which was all over a little too soon when Greta returned.

Harriet smiled, she just had to keep the thoughts that ran through her mind at bay until she met Tustin that evening.

Nick seemed to wobble a bit as he finally stood up.

'Butterfingers,' said Harriet.

'My mistake,' said a pale Nick.

Harriet noticed a little trail of blood through the

ripped trousers. The knife may have been a little blunt, but she'd done her best.

'Adapt and overcome.' As Mother had instructed her girls.

Oh dear, I do hope everything is Ok,' appeared Greta.

'A little clumsy,' mouthed Harriet and made sure her chair pushed against his leg as she stood up to leave.

'Goodbye and thank you,' she trilled warmly in a loud voice.

And Greta remarked what a fine considerate young woman she'd become.

'That was kind to whisper dear, I always find that man a little heavy-handed, maybe there's a bit of trouble.'

Harriet hoped he washed his hands before he buttered anyone else's toast and they left.

Once they had reached the house, Harriet offered to take the shopping inside whilst Greta went to feed the ducks in the park.

'Such kindness today.'

It was something that she and Henrich had so enjoyed. She loved nature and wildlife and the park in a little way reminded her of the countryside and of her home. Besides it was a beautiful day and she needed to be in it. She was alive, and she didn't have many pleasures left to her but being in the park on a day like today was one of them.

Greta had a stash of stale white bread in a brown paper bag stuffed in her coat pocket. And when she sat on one of the benches she couldn't resist opening it up and taking a little bite from one of the chunks. Somehow the staleness suited the fresh cold air and it tasted delicious. She dropped some crumbs on her coat and as she was brushing them of her lap she thought she recognised the two pairs of feet in brown lace up boots that were very quickly marching past her.

It had to be the twins, their boots were rather

distinctive. As she looked up, they had already rushed past, quick stepping in time with one another.

'They must have missed me, I suppose I was bending down,' thought Greta.

Instead of jumping up and running after them, she decided to sit and watch them on their path. They stopped at the aviary. Of course, the birds were their new-found fascination. Greta found the aviary quite a depressing structure, an old Victorian wrought iron building with a blue roof and white painted trim, which always reminded her of icing on a cake. All very beautiful but housing all those trapped birds, which in Greta's opinion should be wild and living in the trees. And there were certainly enough of them in this town, trees everywhere.

She watched the girls take out their notebooks and crayons and watched them as they studied their subject, the concentration etched in their faces. They would be there for hours, not noticing the cold. She looked at the other people in the park and noticed Harriet's friend Tustin, with an older lady arm in arm, taking a slow turn around the borders. She could see that the lady was talking incessantly and that Tustin in comparison, looked grey in the face and subdued. Even at this distance she could see the bags under his tired sad eyes. Her heart went out to him, he'd suffered greatly, and it still continued.

'Well, that's obviously his mother's sister.' And the carer becomes the cared for, which is so often the case.

He reminded her of Guy, whom she had such a fondness for. But she knew that she couldn't fix anything, as she had her own sadness to try and cope with it. It remained in question if she and Guy could help each other. She rather hoped that they could. But today, she wouldn't even think about such things, today she would try and be joyful.

A little girl came over to her whilst she was feeding the swans and they shared the bread throwing, seeing how far each other could get their pieces. She reminded her of Harriet.

'I bet I can get my piece onto the island.'

'Bet, I can go further.'

It was a shame they couldn't have children. She and Henrich had so wanted it, but it wasn't to be. 'Not God's will.' Apparently. People thought her a spinster by choice and pitied or hated her for it. Rarely did any one bother to ask her why these days now that she was getting older. If she was honest, she preferred it that way. It used to stab a little bit somewhere deep within when the mean and gossipy and smug and stupid, would so cheerfully ask.

'Selfish.' They used to whisper.

'So very tragic.' They would say to her face.

'How will you continue with life without purpose?' They would say to justify their own decisions.

'They are the meaning for life.' said the smug yet miserable.

'The only reason for a marriage.' said the ignorant.

But, back then Greta didn't feel at all tragic and she hated them for trying to make her feel that way. Greta and Henrich weren't 'less' or small, they were fantastic. Their very purpose and reason in the world was love. It had been so simple. So glorious.

It was different now.

'My husband is dead.' And it was this absence of love that was the real tragedy.

Her body used to ache at the loss. But now she mostly just sat and stared into space.

Besides she was too old now anyway and maybe God was right not to allow such a travesty. She gulped back a tear that had lodged itself somewhere in the back of her throat, the place where she often felt a little pain.

'I must go now little one.'

'Bye, bye, thank you for the bread.'

It was painful to think that really she was quite alone in the world. She had a sister in Germany whom she couldn't visit. To be honest she had always had dubious far right leanings and they had never been compatible. The only person she had truly loved with every fibre of her being was gone. Her great love was dead and she doubted if she really wanted another, did she?

'It won't be long.'

She had Milly the cat and she liked to think that the children of the big white house cared something for her. Greta hoped to always know Harriet and Guy, but there was a distinction. The twins made her consciously aware that she wasn't family, she was there to assist them and that was that. They often felt they had to remind her of it.

Greta did not think of her old age often, couldn't imagine it possible. Not many people of her generation ever did. It seemed such a luxury. Maybe if she was lucky Harriet would visit her if she was fortunate enough to carry on existing. She had few material possessions weighing her down so that would be straightforward.

'I would rather be with you sooner my love.'

'There is no rush.'

She popped to the tea house after a promenade around the park. The fountains were in full play and she laughed as some of the spray hit her face, the cold sharpness of it made her feel alive. She had a Lyons cake with lemon icing, which was such a treat and a small pot of tea served in a floral china cup. It was cheerful and an act of hope on her behalf. A man in a bright blue suit smiled at her, and because it was a sunny lovely day she smiled back.

She suspected she was still a little beautiful. She hadn't quite tipped into an overlooked and disregarded middle age.

There was life after all.

When she got home all was quiet, so she went to the kitchen and started to prepare dinner. On the side was a bunch of violets which was sweet.

'Harriet must have picked them for me to make me smile.' What a very thoughtful girl.'

'Intoxicating sweet smell, little violets delicate and well, full of secrets that we mustn't tell.'

CHAPTER 11

After dinner and after Uncle William had retired and Guy had been given his medicine, Harriet quickly changed into her father's clothes, which was her new best thing. She didn't put on a bra or shirt as was usual under the waistcoat and her breasts only just fitted in behind the material, battling with the constraint. She undid one button and they were slightly exposed.

'How marvellous,' she thought and did it up again. It could be something to show Tustin later.

They met as usual under the clock tower, Tustin circling a key ring around his finger as she arrived, just waiting for her to ask what it was for.

She tried to resist and act nonchalant, but just couldn't stop herself jumping up and down to grab at it.

'Come on Tust give me the key, you know you want to.'

'Dearest Harry if only I could, but that would simply spoil all my fun.'

They rolled together for a moment, Harriet on the pretence for reaching for the key and Tustin enjoying the soft flesh he felt pushing against him. Laughing and jostling and both feeling slightly embarrassed but loving the physical contact at the same time. Maybe he could feel loved again thought Tustin, whilst Harriet's thoughts were of a much more basic need.

'Don't waste time girls, seek and conquer,' said Mother in her head.

'Hey you two, what are you up to?'

Hilary bounded over and Harriet tried very hard not to look disappointed. She sat up and the three of them sat in awkward silence waiting for their fourth member. Tustin promising to tell them all when he arrived.

It seemed to take an age for Jack to arrive and when he did he joined them on the step and the four just sat there, Jack sensing this was the correct thing to do. It was only when the moment had reached the required level of solemnity did Tustin stand up and turn round to face the clock tower and the little wooden door that stood at its base. He turned the key with great gravitas and opened it.

'Welcome to Netherland.'

A suitable pause.

'Well, it is getting a little chilly now gang, thought you'd appreciate a little bit of warmth.'

The girls gasped and Jack slapped him on the back.

'Oh good job man.'

Giggling the four of them rushed inside and shut the door. The thing that most struck Harriet was the quiet, which was in very stark contrast to the noise of the park outside. The wind rustling in the trees, the quacking of the ducks, the song of the swans, the water bubbling down the weir, the knocking together of the little wooden boats on the river and the odd sound of a cat patrolling. Not to mention those wretched birds shut up in that vile little conservatory.

The drama of their surroundings made the girls whisper in anticipation, and the boys were quite quiet, each taking one of the girl's hands in theirs.

They had landed on a dirty concrete floor and were faced with a wooden vertical sweep of stairs leading goodness knew where.

'Is it safe' asked Hilary.

'Up here?' asked Harriet

It was with some trepidation that they put their feet on the steps and followed Tustin up the stairs. The higher they got, the more she realised she could hear the workings of the clock. Tick, tock, clank clang as the heavy iron seconds made their way around. Each minute seemed to take an age, time suspended.

It was very rare that one ever stood stock still and actually listened to the passing of time, but that evening four young troubled souls did and it made them tremble.

'Time is galloping ahead of us and I can't stop it reaching its terrible conclusion,' said a thoughtful and nervous Hilary.

She thought of death and dying quite a lot and felt the horror of it just waiting for her.

'Well if one lingering moment in time is all we have, then I'm going to make damn sure to enjoy every last moment,' said a trembling yet triumphant Harriet.

'We are alive and present.'

Jack, forever in the moment, didn't say a word and Tustin, well aware that lost time can't be regained, remarked tellingly,

'My parents will never return to me, I'm quite alone. Maybe through the powder I can see them again and track them down.'

'You can at least forget, even if you don't find them this time.' and Harriet placed an arm through his.

'We will find them soon.'

That evening in the clock tower, in the murmuring park, time was suspended. And at that very moment, past, present and future were all there existing together.

'It is the person that can choose to move between time at will.'

'We can beat time, tonight we are travellers.'

'Tonight we are free.'

'Who knows, what we will see.'

Harriet took in the tower room. The workings of the clock were in the corner and the stairs came out into the middle. The moonlight streamed through the clock face windows and it was quite light at the top. Some old garden chairs had been placed around an old copper bowl that looked like it held the remains of a fire. Tustin had obviously been in and added some candles, she recognised that brass candlestick from his mantelpiece at home. Blankets were piled up in a corner and a flask of tea perched on a wooden crate, with Tustin's mother's best gold-plated cups and saucers.

'Well said Tustin, 'she has no need of them now, well does she?'

Each took a seat and a blanket, and they lit the candles and the fire, it was really terribly atmospheric. Harriet felt that this moment would stay in her mind for a very long time. Tustin served them tea and they raised a toast;

'To time.'

'That most persistent of bastards!'

They laughed and took a good slug of hot sweet tea. Tustin then moved behind the clock mechanism and returned with the box in the spirit of eternal escapism. He beckoned to Harriet and she lifted the lift knowing that soon she would be so gloriously happy and feel even more love for her friends than she did at that moment, if that was at all possible.

'Time to escape.'

Tustin solemnly took the blanket away from around her shoulders and faced her. Harriet decided to take a chance and undid the top button of her father's waistcoat. Tustin swallowed but regained his composure and dabbed some powder on the chest that was presented to him.

Jack came over to the pair and took out a pound note

that he rolled in front of them. Harriet could see that the glimpse of her breasts had excited him and in the spirit of now, undid the remaining buttons.

Tustin solemnly and slowly, took the offered rolled up note and placed it on one breast and then Harriet beckoned to Jack, who didn't need to be asked twice. He moved to the other side, moved the material gently out of the way and took a long breath in. Harriet felt exquisite. A moment of abandon. As Tustin watched them, he smiled and licked the remaining dust clean off her now fully exposed chest. Harriet kissed both boys on the head and leant back, allowing their lips to reach up to her neck and back again. The three were quite preoccupied in their pleasure forgetting about Hilary who was left watching them.

They turned when the sound of her chair motioned them to look. She had undressed, and her pale skin shone in the moonlight. She was sitting just as she had been, legs crossed, and looking straight at them. It was Harriet that walked over to her and placed a line of powder on her bare thigh as was their norm. Separating Hilary's legs to be able to then sit in between them, Hilary smiled and stroked her hair as she inhaled. Harriet then reciprocated and offered a powdered arm to her friend.

They hugged afterwards and that made the boys gasp, then Harriet returned to her blanket left on the floor and she sat with Tustin holding his hand as they waited for their hit. It was an excitable Jack who now took the box and went over to Hilary. He stood in front of her and she opened the box and dipped her fingers in the powder and placed them one at a time into Jacks mouth.

Unable to contain himself anymore, he undid his trousers, his erection clear to the room. Harriet and Tustin began to slowly kiss as they watched their friends and Hilary signalled her acquiescence. Jack listened for the tick tock of the clock and rhythmically pushed inside.

It was excitable and quick and took everyone by surprise. He offered up another line to Hilary who gratefully snorted and she in turn offered a dab of powder on her lips for him.

As the clock chimed, the noise almost unbearable they moved together and stood in a group hug, all embarrassment gone and the beginning of a night none of them would forget.

'No shrinking violets, girls.' said Mother.

'A good girl is a terribly bored girl.'

Hilary and Jack dressed and Harriet did up father's waistcoat, happy it had had the desired effect. They laughed and jumped down the stairs, banging the door shut as they went. They went to the bridge and began their climb.

'I can always get higher.'

'Come on you're not even trying.'

CHAPTER 12

❊

Back at the big white house, Guy was alone in his chair when he heard the noise. He'd had a little too much port that evening alongside his medicine, so it took him a while to get up and investigate. When he reached the hallway he was surprised to find it quiet but what was that? Oh no! Not that unmistakeable sweet smell of violets again.

'Mother it must stop, I am tired.'

Her picture looked out at him, surprisingly expressionless, but he could feel her in the house again. He thought that he had 'sorted' that problem out but apparently not well enough.

'My treasure trove.'

He went into the kitchen and as expected the bunch of violets were there again above the sink. It looked like Greta had put them in a vase this time. Or was it Greta? Was it just a coincidence that the vase was the one he had brought for his mother when he was just fourteen? That eventful birthday he very much wished, he could permanently erase from his memory.

He took them out and put them in the bin. Then washed out the blasted vase and concealed it in a different place to the one he had chosen last time as a hiding place.

'Why don't you just smash it?'

'Mother please, it's only going to be put away.'

'Smash it.'

'Please Mother.'

The room grew silent and he shut the kitchen door and made his weary way up the stairs to his room.

Streaking past him like a bolt of lightning, zoomed a piece of rust. Zoom, zoom, zoomity zoom.

His room was sparse compared to his sisters and he liked it that way. Guy didn't want memories of his parents, his French family or anybody getting in the way of his attempts to sleep. Yet, still he saw all their faces over and over again, making it impossible.

He had a picture of his wife and child tucked into the corner of his favourite book, 'L'Assommoir' by Zola. He had it placed in-between the pages, so it was cosseted on both sides. Guy didn't want his sisters to find it, so he changed the position each night. They were not to be trusted.

'We know everything Guy, everything.'

Occasionally he would switch it to his collection of poetry, but the temptation to place it between the bitter sweet words of Keats 'La belle dame sans merci' and Byron's 'Ode to beauty' was all too much, and he felt sure his sisters would discover it there. Didn't want them to discover his secret, which was, that he loved his daughter more than his life. How special she and his wife eternally were. Their beautiful faces were for his eyes alone and he wanted them kept safe that way.

Guy also had a reading lamp by his bedside, on a little wrought iron table he'd found in the conservatory. It reminded him of the outside table and chairs they had owned on the island. It was his nod to memory.

Other purely functional items included a wardrobe and chest of drawers. In fact on first entry to the room, it could have been anybody's. There was little to personalise it and that was the way he liked it.

He lay down fully dressed as he often did, thinking that if he tricked his mind into believing that he was staying awake, it would perversely make him sleep. This was a new technique suggested to him by Dr Abbott, whom Guy wasn't totally convinced had ever trained in medicine at all and didn't care. He was always happy to sign the prescriptions and take the money, so in that way he was a great help and first class.

As he turned his head he disturbed the small purple flower that must have been lying behind his pillow. He didn't jump up or move but nodded his head in acceptance. In resignation and exhaustion, the quiet tears began to fall down his cheek. She just wouldn't let him be. He took an emergency gulp of port and hoped she would go away.

'Please Mother.'

Eventually he fell into a laudanum induced fitful sleep and he saw both his parents calling to him and holding out their arms. Willing and persuading him to join them, their smiles fixed on their faces, their eyes turning cold as he turned his back.

He always thought it strange that violets were his mother's favourite flower, they were so dainty and so delicate, that they seemed so terribly at odds with everything his mother was. She was forever telling them all, that because her birthday was in February and violets were the flower for that month, that their clever father had begun the tradition of decorating the house with them.

'He is so terribly in love with me.'

'Who can help him?'

One tea time, when they were having their nursery tea, of marmite toast, cheese slices and apple boats, Mother interrupted their conversation. If he remembered rightly, it was a very important talk, discussing the virtues of the

Chelsea bun v. the simple iced bun. The interruption infuriated him.

He could picture her clearly sitting in the room. She had a new little silver brooch which had been shaped into a mini bouquet vase, into which she had put the tiniest of little violets. She was terribly pleased with it.

The story, of course could be related back to her, as they always were. Clutching a book dramatically to her chest, she very carefully moved aside their toast (which annoyed Guy, he was hungry!) and with great reverence she opened up the Greek myth book and began.

The story was about Diana's nymphs and about how delicacy was a byword for the violet.

'Wasn't Daddy clever to find a flower that so suits my sensitivity?'

'Purity and delicacy, clever Daddy.'

The pictures in the illustrated guide made the children gasp and he remembered Charity blushed and Grace started to nervously giggle but he was transfixed. The nymphs had their tops off and Apollo seemed to be chasing them with a large erection.

He shuddered as he remembered Mother's hands lingering on the page, her fingers tapping over Apollo. It felt strange and he didn't really understand why. It was also the first time he had seen a naked breast and remembered that he had to suppress a giggle, as the twins drank in every word their mother said.

They were all stunned and amazed at the images before their eyes. As mother got more excited telling her story, she grew redder and redder and he noticed how her stomach rested on her legs, now that she had mostly taken to her bed and couldn't stop eating. It made him feel embarrassed.

'Can't we eat now?'

But Mother had continued. One of Diana's nymph companions was being pursued by her twin brother

Apollo, but they had all sworn loyalty to Diana and that meant that they would forever remain maidens. To protect the girls and their modesty, Diana changed them into violets and that was why chastity, modesty and delicacy became properties of the flower.

'How appropriate,' gushed their mother and the twins clapped in delight as the story came to fruition. But, even as a little boy Guy knew that chastity, modesty and all the rest, were about as far removed from a description of their mother's attributes as any.

'Indulge in legends my darlings.'

Diana was Harriet's middle name.

Guy's mind drifted in its medicinal state and he remembered another time during the war. All around the village was death and destruction. You could smell the putrid reek of death. It went deep down, tickling at your lungs making you splutter and retch.

The only building that was left even slightly standing, was the beaten-up smashed wreck of the little village church. He could hear the church bell now as it dangled precariously by only one wire. It was just waiting to drop and lie in the ground, smashed like everyone and everything else. It eerily rang out as the boys passed by.

'Ding donnnng, ding donnnnng.' In an offbeat sorry key.

He was meant to be in charge, which was hysterical. His rank given because of his family, there was no other good reason and he was ill equipped for the task to put it mildly. He wasn't more than a child. A sensitive soul at that.

To negate this ridiculous truth, he had in effect given over control to his NCO, Jock. Jock was a solid man and understood the situation they were in and played his part well. In front of the men he asked Guy's opinion, and went with it, but Guy had already taken his advice and they had a strong and understanding bond. The war was the kind of necessity that meant men of class and those of ability needed to come together. It didn't always work out and there was much bitterness in some cases.

Guy was lucky, if anyone in the God awful war could ever be considered able, it was Jock.

It was this secretly designated leader, who had decided the church was as good a place as any to take a break. The decision based on the fact that there may be safety in a few standing walls, it could mean they would survive for another day at least.

Guy wasn't about to disagree. They had been abandoned by anyone of any higher rank or real importance, so Jock was the expert.

Guy smiled a weary smile. Jock was a life saver in a very real sense of the word - strong, capable, coarse, angry, and blustering red faced Jock. Not much older than Guy, but something about him made the others trust him. He liked a drink and a singsong, 'Auld Lang's Auyne' being his favourite, it didn't matter that it wasn't New Year's Eve, as Jock used to say:

'Every fucken day we're alive sonny is like bleedin New Year.'

Now, whenever it was New Year's Eve, Guy raised his glass to Jock, wherever he was. That was the thing about the war; occasions such as Christmas, New Year and birthdays always without doubt took you back there, back to the great fucking war.

It was never really out of his mind at the best of times, but especially poignant at those times. He had heard that Jock had survived the war and survived it well. He had gone back to Glasgow and now had a family. Guy was pleased, expected his children would be brought up under the strictest management! But with a warm good-hearted father. He kept meaning to go and see Jock, but he couldn't face any reminders and what would Jock think of him now – that terrified him.

He remembered the colour of that bell especially, the bruised turquoise copper shining in the grey sky. It had reminded him of the bandstand at home that was always painted a cheery glossy shade of eau de nil. He imagined the band, all dressed up in their striped jackets and dickie bows and boaters, singing in that burnt out wreck in France.

Cheerfully stepping over the mess that death dared to make to their boating shoes.

'Oops a daisy.'

He slept for a while, in the big white house with the green door. The sound of the bell and the imaginary band lulling him into a dreamy distant remembrance. It didn't last long, but instead of his mother, he saw his beautiful little girl; Unity. Her mother's blonde hair being twirled around her chubby gorgeous fingers. It was enough to soothe him for a little bit while the bad thoughts disappeared. She often came to him like this, at moments when the bad thoughts began to encroach.

'Papa.' And that little giggle.

It seemed to gain him a bit of strength with which to fight or ignore his demons. He was sure she watched over him. It seemed to give him a bit of hope. She was very much within him.

Once he was a little restored and settled, his mind went back to the church with its beautiful copper bell. They had fallen onto three remaining pews, Guy was lucky to be at the end of one and he rested his head back on the end. As he looked up he saw a beautiful chipped fresco.

Sure, it had bullet holes littered all over it and bits of white plaster showing through, but somehow the bulk of it remained. It was such an unlikely beauty to be found in that place and he had been transfixed.

There was mother Mary, in a bright, lapis blue gown, red hair shimmering down her side vibrantly contrasting with the dress. But it was her face that struck him the most, she seemed to be looking directly at him, a knowing smile on her face. Knowing and accepting and kind. It had been a long time since Guy had seen such a heart-warming sight and he remembered how he had wished the figure had been real. Oh, how he wanted the Madonna to reach out a hand for him to hold.

'All is safe, all is well.'

As exhaustion took hold of him, he held onto the image and it gave him some comfort. He was awoken by Jock with a jolt sometime later. He had no idea how long he had slept, but day had turned to night and it was bitterly cold. He could see the stars through the massive hole in the roof. It was a clear moonlit night and he watched the moon resting for a moment on her serene and lovely face.

'Mother loves the moon,' came the unwanted thoughts. And he saw his mother tilt her face up to the light in that big white house.

As a cloud passed over the Madonna she disappeared momentarily and so he leant down to tie up his boots. Not that they were hardly worth wearing anymore given the state they were in. Covered with rips and holes and as caked in mud as his dreams.

Looking up again for a fond farewell, he noticed that the light had shifted a little showing her hands. He remembered the disappointment still. That feeling of betrayal, the way his stomach seemed to rise into his mouth, the way he had to spit out the bile rising from his empty guts.

In her hands she carried a bunch of violets and he saw the Latin words for humility and modesty written at her feet.

'I'm always with you, dear heart.'

'Mummy is here.'

Jock was busying everyone along and Guy was first

out of the church. It was time to move on out, the sound of shelling nearby making it essential. Jock had begun a round of Auld Lang's Syne and the boys began to whistle. He couldn't join in this time, couldn't make his mouth make any sort of sound as they ploughed out into that cold starry night.

He remembered back to when the twins were little and how they had loved an illustrated book of Shakespeare's Hamlet. He could vividly remember the picture of Ophelia lying floating in a river with wildflowers around her, which included poppies and violets. They were told that violets were a symbol of a heroic death. The girls loved this picture and he often found the book lying open and the twins would make various copies of the image. They would be found strewn all over the house.

They took to garlands of wildflowers draped around their necks.

'Embody your art darlings.'

Their favourite Ophelia series of paintings replaced the young girl's face to an idealised picture of their mother. Mother of course adored these paintings and encouraged the detailed paintings they were now well known for.

'Ahh to dream of violets my girls means good fortune is coming your way.'

'Like Ophelia, I'll always be with you, never forget that my dears.'

Ophelia was Harriet's third name.

He also remembered overhearing his father and his friend from London discussing violets. He seemed to recall that his father began buying their mother the small delicate flowers because the girl he loved as a young man shared the same name.

'Violet, fine filly, good solid cheery thing.'

'Had her under the apple tree on the lawn.'

'That must be why they are so juicy.'

He bet that Mother never knew that. It seemed incredibly spiteful how his father smiled and scoffed. Each gift of flowers, each book, each picture, a mockery that he enjoyed no end. Mother even thanked him each time. A cruel joke.

His father was a bastard.

Of course the children had all carried on the tradition and mother was presented with many a variety of violet on her birthday. Grace had even once tried to grow them in the greenhouse, she had a grand plan of planting them in a giant M shape. Poor Grace, it didn't take off, she was told that pests in the soil had destroyed them. It wasn't true, Guy had seen his father drunk one night go into the greenhouse and tear them up with his hands laughing as he went.

'Violet, my true love, Violet my dove.'

Another theory that he read many years later, was that violets were a sign of death and resurrection.

Resurrection, he used to think it an impossible fancy. He wondered now. He knew better.

His pitiless father was nothing if not a good liar, and no one ever suspected a thing and only Guy knew of his father's love. Guy understood that it was pointless telling them the truth, he would be the one to suffer far more than his father.

'Tittle tattle.'

'Liar, liar, pants on fire.'

Of course his mother somewhat took advantage of her 'special' boy and made him a needy and shy child. Hoping to keep him this way forever, so she could always have him close by. She wanted a man that doted on her and most importantly felt a sense of duty, and it helped that he needed her. He could see that now, but not at the time, never at the time.

His relationship with his father was strained:

'Infernal little Mummy's boy.'

'Pansy.'

This contributed to his very poor self-confidence, but it made Mother giggle and smile and ruffle his hair.

'My darling little pansy flower come to Mummy and she'll make it all better.'

It was the war that helped his relationship with his father. Father of course, due to his class had been given a position of some importance in France, overseeing a large group of men. Utterly unqualified in real terms of course, although it could be argued that no one was really prepared for the horrors of war.

Yet this was a man who bullied and lied and treated his own family with a contempt that was special to the Victorian man. This was a man that was asked to look after a group of mere boys, children sent to die, sometimes even without a weapon or any means of defence. Thank God, thought Guy, that he hadn't been positioned with him.

Compassion and understanding were really never within George Ansell's makeup. He was a man happy to take the spoils of war, drinking champagne when a few feet away his men were drinking contaminated water, or if they were lucky the cheapest nastiest beer they could find. He used to hear them crying, see them shaking and he offered no support at all. He was just like many of the others, and the men faced his wrath:

'Are you men or boys?'

'Stand up and fight damn you.'

And then he would return to his tent, where a meal would be served on army issue china, with silver cutlery and flutes of wine. Guy could imagine it, he'd seen it himself from the other side and felt keenly the sense of abandonment and hopelessness. A few of his group had been shot when they complained. His friend John was shot after he ran the other way over the trenches in a blind panic. It made no sense to him, it sickened him. It made him ashamed of his name and his privilege.

He at least fought with the men. They were the real heroes, if anyone could ever be considered in that way in all this mess. It wasn't cut and dried to him, he saw the faces of the young Germans equally terrified. People died in the same painful twisted sinewy way, covered in mud, in a field in the middle of nowhere, no matter where they came from.

He despaired of this life.

It was the constant mocking and suggestions of weakness that made Guy one day walk up to the desk at the Parish Church and willingly enlist. He was only seventeen. Father was already at the front and sent a telegram congratulating his son.

'Just what a Leighton boy should do.'

It was the only thing he could remember his father ever praising him for. His mother of course was quite hysterical, the twins calmly accepting and Harriet, who was just a baby, simply cried at him all day, which was probably the most accurate and sensible approach.

He got a commission of course, on account of his name and his father and his standing in society. It meant little to him, he knew he was most likely less qualified than many of the men he would fight with and try to command. Fighting, tough warrior men, of which he knew little. Men who had fought all their lives, for food, for drink, for everything they held dear.

For him it was about removing himself from his situation and he would do whatever it took to do just that. He simply didn't understand.

He gave a sad smile to himself now of course, his naivety, his innocence. It was no escape. It was straight to the jaws of hell itself.

The bells they sing their sad refrain
Amongst the monstrous shells that fall like the rain
Within my friends and my loves that pierces and causes
such pain
Like cattle we drive over and over again
Whipped against sense, the blood calls out this terrible
stain.

And they were stained, perpetually stained.

Mother had taken to her bed for a whole week and refused to see anyone apart from Guy, with whom she would plead and cajole and beg, once even on her hands and knees not to go.

'What will I ever do without you?'

'Who will look after my needs?'

She emerged with dark eyes and dressed in black on the day he was to march down the Parade with the new band of the Warwickshire's off to the front.

Many of the town were surprised to see the Leighton's. The girls were also made to wear black and they stood out as usual. They stood motionless, no one was allowed to wave or cheer.

'He must know the harm he has caused girls.'

Conversely, the crowd around them let go in all their patriotic flag waving glory. Mother occasionally would sit in the bath chair she'd made the twins pull her in, looking wan and emotional, touching her eyes with a lace hanky every now and again for special effect.

Guy remembered the feeling of walking with the men, for once he felt a kinship, a band of brothers united in an aim, and for once in his life he felt safe and protected.

Had he felt that way recently? No. Definitely not.

'Dear, reckless pansy.'

He watched his mother and sisters and he didn't feel

sad or worry or despair, in fact he felt enlivened. For once he was free from his mother, free from the big white house and all that entailed.

He only wished he could have grabbed his tiny sister. To this day he had to brush that particular guilt aside.

Guy watched as the twins both took a hand of little Harriet's to hold. It made his pain intensify, but he didn't break ranks and go home with Mummy. For that he was rather proud of himself.

He brushed it away, Pansy wasn't for turning! And he really believed he would be home within the year, with enough knowledge and experience to take her away from them. It would be triumphant.

Guy wasn't to know at that moment, that it wouldn't really pan out that way. So, his primary emotion walking down that street on a summer's day was hope, blinding hope. The sun warmed his cheeks, he had a gang of friends around him, and the once shy nervous boy felt like a man.

CHAPTER 13

It was very different now back in the big old white house, those feelings of hope and warmth had long gone. The fleeting guilt he had felt however, consumed him every time he looked not only at Harriet but the twins too. They were lost to him and maybe if he'd come home sooner, they could have been saved.

'Mummy's angels.'

But they were cold towards him and the only characteristic they seemed to share, was one of a just controlled madness, which was only just below the surface.

They all seemed to have that, it wasn't just the war and his 'little bit of trouble.'

It was true that the war hadn't been what he expected and it hadn't helped him. He didn't feel brave or a 'man' at the front. He felt fear, a blind crazy fear that never abated. In fact, it was still continuing but this time his enemy was his own mind and all of the annoyances. He keenly felt the fear of madness, which only just seemed to be kept at bay. Occasionally it flared up and out.

'Better out than in darling.'

Mother should know.

He managed to sleep some more. In his dreams he was in the kitchen with their dog Timmy, who was licking out a bowl of pastel coloured icing he had placed on the floor. He was thirteen. The gramophone was playing in the drawing room, Mother's voice reached him in waves, piercing through the house, imbedding in the walls, where it would always remain.

'Where's my little treasure?'

Father marched in and threw the small packet of sweets on the kitchen table. They skidded off as they were thrown with such force, and Guy fumbled quickly and only just saved them from falling down the sink. Father walked away laughing. Guy felt indignation rising in his young body and he felt his cheeks flush. He knew how important they were, he'd used all his pocket money to buy them.

Father had told him they had cost his full allowance as they had to be bought from France and he'd had to do a very special deal to get them. It was only now Guy realised it wouldn't have cost a penny, they hadn't come from France and that Father was absolutely and unquestionably a bastard.

Still at thirteen Guy was none the wiser and dried his special sweets very carefully indeed. He heard the alarm clock he had set on top of the cooker and opened the door, to be met with the delicious smell of vanilla and sugar and hot cake, which raced up his nostrils. The steam made his face redden and he inhaled deeply and smiled happily at this delicious confection. Mother would adore his treat.

He gave Timmy a hug in triumph and he wagged his tail and licked his face in agreement. The cakes were a great success. Bigger than nanny's fairy cakes and richer too. He had made buttercream icing flavoured with violet essence. This prized product had been where last month's pocket money had gone. Once he had combined the two by slathering big swathes of buttercream onto the mounds, he waited for them to cool before popping a parma violet sweet on top, the crowning glory and the most expensive sweets he had ever brought. He felt a lump in his throat, they would all be so pleased and proud of him.

He woke at the sound of his parents mocking laughter and sighed. He heard his father mutter;

'Pansy.'

'Darling, he is such a special boy.'

He wiped away a tear and sat back hoping for peace at some point during this very long evening.

CHAPTER 14

❄

The snow came later that week, thick heavy white droves of the stuff, covering all of the town and the white house with the green front door.

The house liked the cold and the house adored the wet.

Slither and zither.

Harriet dashed out into the garden, enjoying the soft coldness fall on her face; she opened her mouth wide to let some of it icily slip down her throat, delicious! Greta saw her from upstairs and dashed down to join her, Milly the cat looking on tentatively.

A snowball appeared from somewhere and managed to get Harriet right on the leg, she dashed behind the water fountain, leaving Greta exposed and giggling. Before long, whoosh! And Greta was shaking snow from out of her hair. Laughing wildly, she ran to join Harriet and the pair armed themselves with compacted snow ready to attack their aggressor.

Guy skated into action along the footpath, now an icy slide and managed in one swift swoop to cover the girls again, leading to more squeals of delight. They took aim and it wasn't long before all three were soaking wet and laughing.

Greta then told them both to lie down and make swooping movements with their arms.

'Snow angels she cried, we are all angels!' The three abandoned themselves to fun, Harriet Diana Ophelia, couldn't remember the last time she'd heard such laughter at home. Her eyes watered and her throat ached with laughing so much. So caught up was she, it took a while before she noticed a pair of boots at her legs. As she noticed them, she saw one reach out and in one deft moment, kick her sharply.

'Owww!'

'Harriet, what on earth are you doing, you will get a chill and we cannot have illness in this house, what would Mother think?'

Another pair of feet arrived and stood by her head.

'Up Harriet, you need to be well.'

Charity was at her shoulders hauling her up.

'Ok, ok, I'll get myself up.'

Greta quickly dusted herself off and stood up, the twins gave her stares as icy as the weather.

'Really Greta, we rely on you to take care of her when we are not here.'

'She is fine, is it so wrong to laugh?'

And with that, without allowing the twins a response she ran into the house blinking quick urgent tears out of her eyes.

Henrich seemed very far away.

Guy lay where he was watching the pantomime play out, Charity sniffed at him and Grace gave him a small wan smile and said.

'It's all right dear we know you can't be expected to know what is right or wrong.'

Guy returned the smile and reached for Harriet's hand;

'Maybe we are more like Mother than anyone.'

With which it was the twins turn to walk quickly inside.

The brother and sister looked at each other in understanding and affection.

'Come on Harry, let's help Greta with breakfast.'

Inside the kitchen, Greta was busying herself with those duck egg plates and was furiously cracking eggs into a mixing bowl. Guy steadied her arm and asked her to set the table. He took over making the scrambled eggs and Harriet smiling to herself began to make the toast, humming along as she did so.

The twins ate little at breakfast, which was unusual for them and pecked at their food, not catching anyone's eye. It was a small victory for the others and Greta smiled as Harriet wolfed down breakfast and even had seconds. This pleased Uncle William especially and seemed to infuriate the twins all the more.

After the meal, Charity announced that she and Grace were going to choir practice at the Parish Church which surprised everyone as it was rare that they even left the house.

'Getting closer to our maker are you girls? Good job indeed, a lot to be said for a bit of religion, aren't you going too Harriet?'

'Uncle, I'm afraid I've already nabbed Harriet to help me with some light bookwork this morning, it's good for girls these days to know how to manage a household, don't you think?'

'Oh very wise Guy, yes quite right, our good lord can no doubt wait.'

Relief flooded over Harriet's face, her sad, distant brother could sometimes, really pull it out of the bag. She was sure he didn't really have any intention of going over any books, she hoped not!

Once the twins and Uncle William had left for the morning, Greta and Harriet wrapped up in their big coats set foot on the new carpet layer of white. Their booted feet crunching deliciously on the snow and making it crackle. They snuggled up arm in arm, their camaraderie fresh from the morning's exploits.

Bread in pockets, they made their way to the park to feed the ducks and swans. They spent a happy morning, feeding the ducks and drinking hot chocolate and for once Harriet felt content. She had no mad desire to rush off to the Cadena cafe, no need to long for Tustin, no need to be at home in case anything happened to Guy. She felt content, right there and then with Greta holding her hand and laughing. There was nowhere else that morning that she'd rather be.

They took the long route back and found some fish scraps to take home for Milly, Greta had decided that today was the day for treats and a little rule breaking.

Harriet Diana Ophelia Leighton knew a lot about that.

Once home, Guy had the kettle on waiting for them, which in itself was quite a surprise. His breath was clear, with no medicinal tang. Knowing what this meant cheered the women even more, if that was possible.

The twins sat in the cold icy church for some time after the service, the rector, a kindly old soul saw them.

'Can I help you at all?'

'No thank you Reverend, we are quietly communicating with our lord.'

'Of course my dears, I shall be sorting out the hymn books, should you need me.'

He irritated Grace, they needed this quiet time away from the house to think and ask questions of a higher deity.

'He may yet have his uses dear.'

It was dark by four in the afternoon these days, the cold winter had begun to settle in and so the lamps had been lit, by the time the girls arrived home after lunching with the Reverend, at his insistence.

'Greta, we'll take tea in the attic room, we have our work to continue with, leave it outside the door would you?'

The others were still in the kitchen, Guy had produced a packet of cards from the drawer. He remembered them as Fathers, and they still smelt faintly of tobacco.

'Let's finish our game first Greta, I'm winning and I've no intention of letting you take this opportunity to steel away my advantage.'

He smiled kindly at her and Greta felt herself blush beneath his gaze. Harriet giggled.

'As if you're winning! And if you are it's only because you're cheating!' they giggled and Guy reached over and started tickling his little sister who squealed in delight.

Greta took the opportunity to boil the water for the twin's tea. Today seemed like a breakthrough.

Unbeknown to them, in the pantry, a chunk of plaster dislodged and fell to the floor.

She made her way upstairs with the tea things, she was feeling benevolent and placed a pretty plate of biscuits on the tray for the sisters. It had been cold, they needed the fuel she thought caringly to herself.

It was quiet in the attic room, she knocked and still there was no sound. She knocked harder and opened the door.

The twins were sitting on chairs holding hands with a spare empty chair. They did not look up or acknowledge Greta at all, in fact they seemed lost in their thoughts. A candle flickered in the dark winter light.

With a new-found sense of unease, Greta made her way down the stairs, Guy and Harriet were still mercifully teasing one another, Harriet's cheeks flushed from laughter. She went to the sink and washed her hands, she felt she needed to after being upstairs, she didn't understand what she had seen and was quite sure she didn't want to.

Advent arrived quickly. In previous years Guy had not wanted to celebrate and the house had been left undecorated. It had seemed to him a gross betrayal of the loved ones he had lost. He felt that the cold and disloyal house somehow didn't deserve to be cheered up.

It seemed ridiculous that winter nights should have some cheer and joy. The twins of course agreed, however they always had a lit candle in front of Mothers' portrait and they asked Greta to provide some greenery for the picture frame. They also insisted on a wreath on the door, which must have a violet in it.

'We are not barbarians, after all.'

They had procured a false one some years earlier and they made it the focal point of their design. For Guy this was difficult, but he thought that as it was outside the house, he didn't need to look at it often.

This year it was different, the house felt more alive, the damp had halted in the main rooms. The veins stagnant, unsure of the lightened mood, the increased warmth. Guy and Harriet were both feeling happier, Guy certainly wondered if he had turned a corner. He was drinking noticeably less and he smiled more.

Harriet watched him with Greta, he was kind with her and she noticed. She began to hope for more. It made her feel safe, the prospect of love from their situation felt extraordinary.

One Saturday he arranged for an expedition to the nearby Cubbington woods. He said they would take a car from Christchurch gardens, at the top of the Parade, to the walkway to the woods. He checked they were all wrapped up warmly, insisted on flasks of hot tea to be taken in a bag and chocolate.

'I would like you to accompany us.'

'But Guy dear we have our work, we shouldn't leave the house.'

'It can wait, it's important, we are family.'

Guy smiled inwardly, it was about time, he made his sisters understand their situation, he had let them rule the roost for far too long, there was to be a change in the guard.

'You can take Harriet of course, the fresh cold air will be good for her complexion.'

'I would like you to come too, I think Mother would expect it.'

He felt no shame in mentioning mother to the girls, he was becoming increasingly annoyed at the twins' isolation. It had never really bothered him before, but he was now more aware than he ever had been. He noticed their absence. He noticed.

'Well if Mother would want it.'

And with that and the promise of finding some holly for mother's picture frame, the girls had no choice but to join the expedition.

CHAPTER 15

Harriet had to admit to feeling a little disappointed with her sisters in tow, but perhaps it would give Guy and Greta some time alone. She must try and make that possible, even if it did mean having to spend some time alone with the twins.

'Ahhh amour amour.'

'It will seek you out my loves, my treasures, my doves.'

So, on a day in December, the family and Greta, locked the door of the white house and made their slow progress up the Parade. They stopped at the war memorial on Euston Place and placed a wreath for their undeserving father. It made Harriet smile, she missed him still and was pleased to remember him. She saluted, she couldn't help herself. She knew Guy didn't like to remember so she made sure she was standing behind him when she did it.

Outside the town hall a group had gathered. A small stall selling hot chestnuts was doing brisk trade and Harriet and Greta both had a bag. Guy playfully stole a few out of each of their packets, whilst the twins looked on in mild disgust. It seemed to them rather common.

'They really don't look clean Harriet.'

'Guy, I do hope Dr Abbott will be available for the undoubtable sickness.'

'Not for us dear, not for us.'

The Salvation Army broke into a roaring rendition of 'Oh come all ye faithful' which they all joined in with.

'Decent folk.'

'And not one of them has a chestnut in their hands.'

As Harriet looked around her, she felt warm and it wasn't just from the chestnuts. It was the joyful fact that her brother was there. Her brother was well enough at long last to join in the celebrations. She saw laughter in his eyes when all she'd really seen since he came home was loss and despair. They spent a good hour singing along and then they made their way up the Parade, past the Cadena cafe and onwards to Christchurch Gardens. Their car was waiting for them and they wrapped themselves up in the blankets provided and continued the next two or three miles warmly and in good spirits.

Greta started her own rendition of silent night, having to keep her well known childhood German words to herself. Still the tune itself transported her back to happier, safer times. Maybe the last time she had ever felt truly at home.

In the blink of a hastily rubbed away tear, she was at home in Germany and the war hadn't happened. There was a tree and she had iced gingerbread hanging on it, just waiting for a bite on Christmas Eve. She gulped, she could taste the cinnamon, the overwhelming sweetness of that first bite of icing. Her mother sang:

Stille Nacht, heilige Nacht,
Alles schläft; einsam wacht
Nur das traute hochheilige Paar.
Holder Knabe im lockigen Haar,
Schlaf in himmlischer Ruh!
Schlaf in himmlischer Ruh!

They went as far as they could in the car and stopped

on the outskirts of the wood. The path ahead had started to freeze and icy glints flickered in the sunlight, giving the walk a sense of wonder.

Guy took Harriet's arm and Greta walked alongside them with a basket picking berries and holly for the Christmas decorations.

'Verdammet'

The blood began to seep out of her finger in little spherical bubbles that captivated the family, who all stood and watched silently for a moment.

'Here Greta, use my hanky.'

It was Harriet who went to her friend's aid and wrapped it up whilst giving her a kiss on the cheek.

'Thank you my little one.'

And with that, Greta took Harriet's other arm and the three of them marched ahead of the twins, who dawdled at the back. Charity now master of the basket, rather haphazardly added items they found on their way.

'We can paint this later, put this in dear.'

'My arms were not designed to carry much Grace.'

'Then give it to me, Guy can take it when we get inside the trees.'

'Best cover this with a little moss then.'

Up ahead, Guy began to hum, 'We wish you a Merry Christmas,' and before long the threesome were singing together compatibly, which made Harriet tingle and feel toasty inside, despite the weather turning chillier with each passing minute.

Suddenly the track petered out and they were faced with a wall of trees, beech, oak and larch. The last of the sunlight was dappling through the green and dark façade. The entrance was narrow and they could smell the fresh earth and mossy smell, Grace breathed in deeply so it filled her nostrils.

'It smells clean.'

'Come along I'll lead the way through.'

A bird disturbed by the humans, swooped from inside and made its call. It was a long mournful wail which left Harriet feeling like they were entering a different and wild world.

Unbidden. Unasked. Unknown.

'Take just one little step and the rest will follow,' whispered Mother.

Inside it was quite dark with only a glint of sunlight allowed to seep through. It reminded Harriet of home somehow. Was it the musty smell and the mossy mildew? It was instantly recognisable and it made her shudder a little.

The house took its opportunity with its occupiers gone, and the damp and the mould started on its inexorable journey once more. Slowly seeping and sating itself.

Creeping and swarming and spinning and suuuucking. Boldly squirming hips-a-swirling.

It was free, which was always the best time to make bold moves.

It was time she thought, to see if she could engineer some moments for Guy and Greta to be alone. She smiled to herself, they would then become like parents for her and she missed having that in her life. That, which she supposed was normal. That, which she had no idea about.

'This and that and that and this. It is, it is, it is.' Murmured through the trees.

Turning around she saw that the twins had disappeared off somewhere. She wished she had sisters she could talk to and accomplices to her very earnest mission. But she suspected they were off inspecting some moss, or wildlife for one of their many projects.

It was time to put her plan into action, so she let Guy and Greta walk ahead of her a little and seizing her moment darted quickly behind a tree.

She felt her heart in her mouth and she breathed quickly and heavily, excited by her game. After a minute she darted back behind her to another tree and stood stock still for a moment more.

No one came, no one called out, so she ran in the opposite direction of her brother, lost to them. Time for them to be alone.

Laughing she came to rest at an over turned tree stump, all around her the trees closed in on her and she felt really truly alone and had a fleeting moment of feeling quite free.

Dancing and dashing here and there, twirling and whirling, toes pointing and fingers waving, Harriet spun in the dwindling light.

Like silk, she slid and pirouetted.

'Drop one hip, roll those shoulders, smoulder and sap their strength girls.'

Spin.

Coming to a stop by the hollow of the tree stump, she saw a dead mouse laid out in his final resting place. She sighed and placed leaves around him to make a pretty grave. As she disturbed him she could see that little insects had begun to eat the one side of his face which gave her a little start. Feeling a little uneasy with this discovery, she wandered off leaving her little friend behind, and as she did so she was surprised to brush a little tear aside.

'Don't be so ridiculous Harry' she admonished herself. What did you expect to see on a nature walk?

Now her head spun.

She took a cursory look around her and of course she saw no one, so she reached into the depths of her pocket and took out the tissue she had carefully hidden within. Out came a stolen cigarette and matches, heavenly. All the more so because she had been so daring to steal it in the first place.

'Top marks for stealth darling.'

'That's my girl.'

Feeling relaxed now despite the cold, the hot smoke from the cigarette comforting and warming, she breathed deeply. She stood stock still to enjoy the illicit pleasure all the more. Above her a group of ravens made there carr, carr carring sound, flitting from tree to tree above her. As soon as she looked up, one swooped to her feet and gave her a watchful eye.

She was always surprised at the size of some of the local birds, ravens in particular with their glossy black beak and beady stare. She remembered a school book and the story of the ravens. In Norse mythology they were said to represent the underworld, a symbol of one's inevitable end.

Odin the God of the Underworld had two ravens called Huginn and Muninn and they served as his eyes and his ears. Huginn represented thought and Muninn, memory. In this way the ravens would fly around gathering information to bring to Odin. It made her shudder a little.

'All seeing little birds eh, taking messages to the Underworld.'

'Tell my father I miss him.'

'Tell Mother I love her.'

It was also Wednesday and that she remembered from school history lessons was Wodens Day, another way of saying Odin. How apt.

She also remembered the Swedish cousin of Hilary's coming to visit some summers ago, they were just children and were camping overnight in Hilary's back garden. They had a little fire and over the toasting of the marshmallows they began to tell ghost stories. Hilary told the local story of Guys Cliffe House and the lady on the balcony whose lover was lost to her and how she stood on that balcony most evenings looking for him, wailing her long dead ghostly wail. Ever since then Harriet had shuddered at the sight of the metal balustrade in amongst the rest of the ruined house.

Harriet's story was one about escaped mental patients causing havoc, and she remembered at the time she pictured her siblings as the patients. The thought of that now cheered her up a bit. It was so silly and yet so apt!

'Tick tock, tockety tick, it won't be long.'

Swedish Agatha began her story of two ravens who were well known to represent the ghosts of murdered people. And if you ever saw a raven they were exacting revenge for the poor tortured souls. Stupid Agatha, and stupid story Harriet told herself out loud. With her stupid blonde hair and pale skin, she had reminded her of her sisters which felt a little chilling.

She wished the thought hadn't lodged itself in her head, it was spoiling her moment.

'Shooh, away with you scary bird.'

The bird stayed stock still, unfearful.

'Shoooh away I say,' with a determined stamp of the feet.

The bird leaped towards her and then flew off back up into the trees above her to watch from a safer distance.

Spooked, Harriet began to run back in the direction she had come from.

Greta and Guy were having a great conversation. They were talking about nonsensical things, things of little importance, their favourite songs, food, and drinks. For both of them it was a welcome break from their usual thoughts of absence and loss. For Greta's part she felt she could actually be in the here and now and that felt exhilarating. Discovering a girlish giggle, she didn't even know her throat could make such a sound, made her laugh all the more. Guy in return had lost track of where they were, who they were with and gabbled on, talking at speed and to such a pleasant and warm audience.

'Is the finger better now?'

He took her hand and slowly unwound the handkerchief. She felt herself gasp at his touch and hoped he hadn't heard it or felt her heart miss a beat.

'I'll just check and then cover it back up.'

With each gentle movement she lost more breath, until she could bear it no more.

'It's fine, thank you Guy.'

And with that he let her hand drop.

'Drop kick darlings.'

'Irresistible.' Whispered Mother on the breeze.

Greta's breathing returned to normal but she felt an incredible sense of loss which rode in waves over her body causing it to ache.

Such an ache, it was palpable.

They reached a clearing near the ancient pear tree, which is when they remembered that Harriet was meant to have been with them.

Harriet was quite out of breath now running through the woods, mud splattered upwards onto her clothes and she felt a gnawing sense of unease.

'Guy?'

'Greta?'

'Guy, where are you, can you hear me?'

Then something caught her eye and she stopped and turned back and began walking towards it. There was something white out there, incongruous in amongst the shades of green and brown and black. The end of the sunlight caught the object and it sparkled for a second before disappearing again. Harriet followed.

'Harriet, dear, you are filthy.'

'Come over her and see what we are doing.'

'Mother wouldn't like to see you looking so muddy, what have you been up to I wonder?'

She felt little relief that at least she wasn't alone anymore.

On a glassy black stone lay the raven, its wing looked as if it had been smashed and the life had gone from those eyes which only a moment ago had been so alert and alive.

'I don't understand, Grace, Charity?'

'Beautiful isn't it dear.'

'Look at its skull, just there, that's where we caught it.'

'Don't worry, we are capturing it quite accurately, just look at the tiny brain fragments.'

'Such complex detailed work takes a tremendous amount of skill you know.'

'Blood can be so beautiful against the black, look Harriet look.'

'Isn't it the most splendid thing?'

Harriet was too tired and cold to cry, too lonely to utter a single word in response. How could she share blood with these people? This was grisly. She simply didn't understand or even to want to try.

'You look pale as well as dirty Harriet, I told Guy it was too much of an expedition for you.'

'You must wait with us whilst we finish.'

'I saw something sparkle, what was it?'

'It must have been the magnifying glass.'

'Maybe it lit up our hair. For some reason we feel like little angels today.'

'It must be because it's nearly Christmas,' laughed Charity.

Sparkle and dazzle.

Harriet returned with a wan smile and wished she hadn't turned around, wished she hadn't seen it at all.

'You see we were trying to get a bit of heat on the bird, to change the colours of the feathers somewhat, it didn't really work, in fact I think we may have burnt a little hole.'

'Silly us, but look at the hole dear, you can see right through.'

Harriet felt sick. 'Why?'

'Why, Harriet, Why, what a silly question.'

'We are artists and we create, just like Mummy expects.'

'Death is terribly beautiful really dear, you shouldn't be afraid, just look at that shade, and see how it looks blue if you turn it.'

'Besides didn't the silly bird scare you?'

At that Harriet turned away and sat a few metres away and thought of Tustin holding her. And when that didn't work she conjured up images of a father she never knew who held her hand and led her out of the woods and into the light.

'Oh, my baby darling girl.' He said.

An hour or more passed as she watched her sisters excitingly draw the poor animal, adding more small degradations along the way, 'to add tone' 'for texture'. But she knew they would have done it anyway for fun.

Finally, they stood up and packed away their art pads and materials. Grace wrapped the raven in the cloth, made the sign of the cross and signalled to Harriet to join them. The three girls walked in silence to the edge of the trees, the ravens were still circling above them, but they were silent now.

To the edge, always to the very edge. Why was that?

As they came to the opening, Harriet picked up her pace and almost sprinted through the other side and out into the open fields. She took a deep breath, she could see the farm at Weston Under Weatherly from where she stood, could see the cows and there was somebody on a horse not so far away. It would be OK.

The twins appeared at either side of her, glowing in the amber rich hues of the dying winter sun. They looked serene, but Harriet wasn't so sure. A noise behind them alerted them to Guy and Greta coming out of the woods, relief spreading over their worried faces.

'Harriet thank goodness, where did you go?'

'I'm pleased you found your sisters, at least you had some company.'

'We had a marvellous time Guy, what a super idea of yours,' trilled Charity.

Guy felt pleased, his outing with his family had been a success, and it was good to see the twins with smiles on their faces.

The five stood in silence and watched the sunset. Vermillion, then crimson to a terracotta sky.

CHAPTER 16

Later that evening after a large meal, which everybody except Harriet consumed with relish, having had such an enjoyable day, retired to the lounge for a festive sherry. Greta and Guy were in such good spirits and full of all-encompassing thoughts of each other that they didn't notice Harriet's reticence. Harriet for her part only agreed to join them for drinks so that she could have some alcohol, she wasn't normally allowed.

'I'll get the drinks everybody.'

'There is a bottle in the dresser Harriet.'

'Yes dear, we should have the good stuff.'

Harriet took the bottle and went into the kitchen to get some glasses; as she did so she saw the basket from the trip on the table. As expected it was full of holly, some ivy, some berries, some fern and moss for the wreath. She lifted the moss to smell its green freshness and from underneath out fell some little dead mice. The space within revealed the poor raven's wing at the bottom of the basket.

She jumped and must have screamed. Or was it inside

her head. She didn't know anymore.

Silent screams had become quite her thing.

'What was that noise did anybody hear that?'

'No Guy dear, not a sound, said Grace 'maybe you had a little too much wine at dinner.'

And with that they all laughed and Grace and Charity smiled at one another.

Harriet took a very large swig of the sherry and carried five generous glasses back into the room.

Her sleep was troubled and Mother visited her more than once throughout the long night.

'All that is left of me, is you.'

...

The days passed without further incident and everyone relaxed.

The rust and damp and blither and dither took to underneath the floorboards. The floorboards that were being danced and swayed upon for the first time in a while.

It was a little Christmas present for the unknowing.

Christmas Eve arrived suddenly and there was an unmistakeable whiff of excitement in the air. They had some more snowfall during the night which made it all the more special. Guy was in better spirits and had allowed the fires to be lit first thing in the morning. He felt hopeful, there was no need to scrimp at Christmas. It was one of the first seasons he had enjoyed for many years. Cinnamon sticks and fir cones covered in mixed spice sat in bowls in the downstairs rooms and the sloes they had picked in the wood had made their way into a bottle of gin in anticipation of merriment.

Tis the season.

Harriet arrived downstairs blurry eyed and smelt

Christmas, before she even opened her eyes and saw the decorations. A bowl of oranges sat on the kitchen table and she dove in, juice covering her arms and face, delicious.

'Harriet there you are, hope you haven't forgotten Midnight Mass?'

'Of course not, I'm looking forward to it this year.'

For once this was true, she was enjoying her Christmas and singing carols in candlelight would make it even more magical and make her feel that she belonged to a happy family who could celebrate together.

'We'll be leaving at 9.30pm prompt.'

'But it starts at 11 Charity, why so early?'

'Confession, Harriet, oh surely you haven't forgotten, we've arranged it especially for you.'

Rubbish, thought Harriet, what a waste of time that would be, still it would be her Christmas gift to her sisters if it meant that much to them.

'And you must be clean dear, so bath at 8.30, I've already told Greta to add some specialness.'

Greta arrived downstairs and busied herself in the kitchen until Charity left.

'Little one, come here, I've a surprise for you.'

And from behind Greta's back came a gingerbread heart, the first year since leaving Germany she had felt confident and loving enough to bake one. There was bright white icing and, in the middle, a big H made out of entwined vines.

'Oh Greta, thank you.'

After looking at it quietly for ten minutes in silent delight, it was demolished in minutes and a restored and happy Harriet was back on track for a special Christmas.

The day passed happily for the family. The twins remained mostly in their rooms, preparing their gifts for tomorrow and deciding on which luminous outfit to wear for mass. One of 'those occasions' that this year even they were looking forward to.

8.30 arrived, as did Harriet at the bathroom, her bath waiting for her. The water was tepid which was annoying, still the sooner she got in the sooner it was over. Before she could lock the door, her sisters arrived and sat themselves down on the side on the bath.

'Come along then dear, off with your clothes.'

'I am quite capable of having a bath alone thank you.'

'We won't stay long dear, just want to make sure you have a proper scrub.'

'You do need to be as clean as possible tonight before confession.'

Harriet shrugged off her clothes and got in, the water sending little goose bumps all over her body.

'Pass me the carbolic soap Grace.'

'No need for that one surely Charity, the Pears is over there and it's so much nicer.'

'We are removing dirt Harriet that's probably built up over a long time.'

'I do wash you know.'

'Just be quiet Harriet, we've still got to ready ourselves you know, don't be selfish.'

At that the sisters scrubbed and scrubbed until Harriet was red raw. Not only was the carbolic soap used but a nail brush used to apply it. The bleach they'd put into the water latched onto the red and burning skin and Harriet began to sob.

'For goodness sake child, don't be such a baby, cleanliness is next to Godliness.'

'Now Charity.'

At which her sister submerged her fully under the water whilst Grace held her legs down fast. Harriet struggled and just when she thought she might drown was brought up spluttering and choking.

'Ahh now that's it. Clean.'

'I think she'll do.'

'Good, you're ready Harriet, now be sure to wear the dress that is on your bed.'

They left the room, shutting the door behind them and Harriet curled up, not noticing the now cold water and sobbed some more.

She must have drifted off, for the next thing she remembered was a knock at the door.

'15 minutes Harriet, what are you doing?'

The three sisters sat in a line in the pew, in the Parish Church that was bedecked in all its Christmas finery. Candles softly swayed and the warm tender glow was in severe contrast to the upright girls waiting to be seen.

The flower arrangements were spectacular, natural bark and chrysanthemums mixed with poinsettias and natural foliage, which Harriet hoped wasn't from the wood. There was a faint smell of incense, a warm spicy scent that should have been soothing and no doubt was delightful to anyone who hadn't been scrubbed in a bleach bath moments before. It made her feel sick and it caught in the back of her throat, far too sweet and cloying.

Intense.

She wanted to scream and yet she sat there quietly, her hands in her lap, looking for all intents and purposes how a Leighton girl should look. The only hint that something was wrong, a glaze in her usually smiling eyes.

Charity and Grace were quick in the confessional booth, Harriet wryly thought that was because they didn't even realise quite how mean they were. No sins to forgive. Add to that their standing in the parish and their impeccable appearance. They looked Godly. Both were dressed in winter white with a fur trim to their hem and neckline and wore Mother's best gold jewellery. They looked what could only be described as spectacular.

'Give them what they expect darlings. Never disappoint.'

'Harriet Leighton.'

She stood up and straightened the purple violet dress that she had been asked to wear. She felt uncomfortable, her red skin itching and raw underneath the satin of the dress. The formality offended her. She'd been dressed like someone far too grown up and like someone who cared. Neither of these things were how Harriet felt.

'I can understand your youthful exuberance Miss Leighton, but you should really follow the example of your sisters.'

'Bring God more into your heart, your sisters will help you.'

When she at last sat back down, the congregation had started to come in, she felt the cool rush of air as the door opened and closed, heard the happy excited voices. The choir started to practice, the boys in their red gowns with the white ruffles were adorable. It should have been perfect. But she wanted to cry.

Then she saw them, Guy and Greta, striding towards them. Did she imagine it, or were they holding hands when they first came in. Maybe that was just wishful thinking. She ran towards them and embraced them, sandwiched herself in-between them, so she wouldn't have to touch either one of her sisters. She would not let them ruin her Christmas.

'Darling girl, what a lovely welcome.'

'I hope you've got your best voice ready for all the carols.'

On cue, the organist struck up 'Oh come all ye faithful' and Guy joined in with hearty gusto, which was enough to make Harriet smile again. And for his part, Guy managed to ignore the ghastly violet dress she had chosen. Perhaps she was trying to look grown up, nothing more and with that thought he gave her arm a playful squeeze. She didn't let go of his arm until the carol had finished.

It was pitch black when they left the warmth of the Church and began the short walk back to the big white house with the green door and its new wreath made with the blood of the raven and the mice.

CHAPTER 17

♥

Christmas Day and Guy awoke early to find Harriet on the stairs talking to the picture of Mother.

'Happy Christmas my darling.'

'I miss you.'

'I'm not far away.'

'I know.'

He kissed her cheek and said jovially

'Happy Christmas Ma.'

Harriet chuckled.

'Happy Christmas Harry.'

'You too brother.'

'Let's get some pre-breakfast, before the others get up.'

With that, they tiptoed into the kitchen and found the shortbread tin and Harriet poured some milk.

'Well it is Christmas.'

They then took a dance around the lounge until they heard movement upstairs and then ran to their rooms like naughty schoolchildren as if they had never been awake.

In her room, Greta was lying in, the cat purring contentedly at her feet. She was awake really but didn't want to open her eyes just yet, wanted to savour her dreams of walking in the snow with Guy, who turned into Henrich and then back again. It wasn't unpleasant she liked being with both of them in dream land.

As she gradually became more and more alert, the cat started to shift in her position and so she lay there a while longer, even if her shoulder was twisted and had started to ache a little; it was Christmas for the cat too after all! Last night at church she had lit a candle for Henrich and told him how much she loved him and missed him. She told him Guy had become a friend but nothing more. She was surprised at herself for lying to him and she wondered if he realised. Did the dead know everything?

The game was beginning to change.

Maybe he was laughing at her efforts, she hoped he would be kind.

'All that will be left will be you.'

She felt a pang of nerves which were also keeping her from jumping out of bed to celebrate Christmas. Greta had made the other children a gingerbread heart just like Harriet's. You could tell that she had put an enormous amount of effort into Guy's and she hoped it would be OK, she hoped he knew that she cared. At this moment she felt embarrassed and it was good that it was wrapped up and under the tree or else she would have hidden his as the time approached.

'Well Milly, Happy Christmas my precious friend.'

Milly snored in response and for once Greta didn't make her bed and allowed her to sleep all wrapped up in the warmth, tangled in the blankets.

She chose the nicest of her three dresses, the one she kept for best, for church or for when Uncle William came to stay. She had knitted herself a colourful corsage, a little like the one she'd seen one of the Mitford girls wearing in the newspaper a few weeks ago. A red rose with a little trim of white had been delicately created, which she hoped was festive and would cheer her appearance up. It had been a long time, since she had cared a jot how she looked. Greta had knitted a smaller flower, which she attached onto her metal hair grip, to carry her 'new look' forward. She stepped back and admired her handiwork.

'Not too bad for a middle-aged Hun eh.'

Especially not for one who'd lost everything that ever mattered to her. She looked full of promise - like a young woman with some life ahead of her.

On that cheerful thought, she made her way downstairs to prepare Christmas breakfast. She laid out the Christmas plates, that in itself was wonderful – no duck egg plates this morning. She found herself humming silent night and felt, dare she say it, but a little bit excited, the nerves dispelling a little.

She didn't see him standing behind her, she felt him first.

'Be irresistible, be unnerving darlings.'

'Happy Christmas Greta.'

'And you too Guy.'

She turned around very slowly, spoke with her back to him, and didn't want her eyes to give her away until she had composed herself a little.

After the turn, she could smile and she saw humour and did she see a little flicker of desire from Guy?

'Greta, you look magnificent! What a cheerful brooch and I love the flower in your hair.'

And with that he reached out and touched it, his hand brushed past her ear, which made her shudder a little and she found that she couldn't utter a word.

Again.

Time was lost and she felt lifted away from the dining room of the white house, with the green front door. Decades soared past, years flew by waving, days and seconds whispered past smiling at her and that moment was simply all there was.

She heard a chair scrape and it brought her unwillingly back. He was still there smiling at her, she was back in the room and he was with her.

'Merry Christmas brother.'

'Greta, season's greetings.'

An icy cold kiss brushed past her cheek, her hands gripped with a vice like precision.

'Happy Christmas Charity.'

This time she could brace herself for the rush of cold.

…'Grace, Merry Christmas.'

'Let me help you in the kitchen, Greta, we will all pitch in this Christmas, won't we girls?'

They left the room, before the silence became deafening.

Harriet was beyond bored, longing for it to be the next day, when she'd be able to sneak away and see the gang, feel Tustin's lips against wherever she didn't care much, as long as it was somewhere.

They were listening to gramophone records before lunch, the twins sketching of course. Greta was gazing absent mindedly into the fire and Guy was so impossibly cheerful, it was the only thing that made the scenario bearable.

'Come on little one, I need a dance partner.'

'Guy, I'm tired, leave me alone, and get one of the twins to dance.'

'Nonsense, come on chickadee.'

And with that Harriet was waltzed around the room, which eventually made her smile and a long-lost memory eeked its way from a hidden part of her brain and she found herself in Mummy's bedroom and that song was playing and Mother was laughing…

'Oh Guy, you're irrepressible.'

'Such big words little sister,' and with that he danced

her back to her seat.

Dinner passed by quite pleasantly, the twins even seemed to be enjoying themselves. They had a goose from Home Farm, Graces' choice.

'They assured me their man had shot it himself, clean in the neck, no shot to chomp on.'

'Just imagine that, a clean shot, quite difficult.'

After dinner, it was the time for presents and Greta gave Guy his gingerbread heart.

The sisters exchanged glances.

'I hope you enjoy it Guy, it's an old family recipe.'

'Thank you Greta, what a treat.'

They both ignored the words she had expertly crafted on and as he snapped it in two to share a little hairline crack appeared somewhere within Greta's heart.

In a house full of cracks this wasn't unusual.

And the house laughed.

CHAPTER 18

The next day the family had been invited to yet another festive 'dreadful occasion'.

There was to be a Boxing Day Hunt, the thought of which turned Harriet's stomach. Poor Mr Fox! It was being held at the Lyles of Eathorpe's lodge, followed by a drinks and dinner reception at nearby Wappenbury Hall. It was considered as one of the highlights of the Warwickshire country calendar and one of the very few that the twins wished to attend. And one that wasn't quite so dreadful but quite the occasion.

'Diamonds and pearls dears.'

They loved the hunt, the chase, the blood, oh that wonderful smell! Grace especially loved it. She'd never forgotten her first hunt as a teenage girl and the blood of the fox smeared on her face afterwards. Father thought it was 'absolutely necessary' and the deed carried out with great gravitas.

'Let's see how tough my little girls are.'

Some had caught her lip and she'd automatically

licked before she realised the fox's blood would be in her mouth. It was delicious, that rich iron taste, salty strong and sublime. She looked at the animal at their feet and felt a sense of triumph.

No, the Leighton girls didn't baulk at the sight or taste of blood or death, not like their ridiculous contemporaries, girls who fainted and cried and welled up with emotion, silly stupid and facile.

'That's my girls.'

They weren't looking forward to the party afterwards but that was to be expected. They would do what was necessary, what Mother expected them to do.

'You need to learn how to sparkle darlings.'

'Put your best dress on and the most daring lipstick.'

'You are young and irresistible. Go forth.'

Guy too, with his new found enjoyment of life and his desire to cement his family closer together agreed it was right that they all go.

The twins had asked Greta to make sure that their finest ball gowns would be ready for the evening reception. They had opted for matching outfits, the same pearlescent ice blue, which of course suited their paleness perfectly; the small hint of crystalline turquoise matching their eyes.

'I am the brother of ice queens.'

'Oh Guy, how silly.'

'Absolutely correct.' The girls thought in private. They knew it was a strong and intimidating look. There was gravitas and bliss in that.

'And you will be unstoppable.' Whispered mother.

Harriet paid little attention to the preparations and as such had the same violet dress on that reminded her of the dreadful Christmas Eve bath and confessional box. Greta was not invited and although she would have loved to dance with Guy, feel his body close to hers, his hand gently resting on her waist, his breath close to her face; she understood the English rules of society and did not wish to burden him with controversy. The German 'frau' would not be understood, would not be welcomed.

Plus, she was looking forward to an evening to herself so that she could quietly think about Guy and what he was becoming to mean to her. And she couldn't think whilst he was in the house because just seeing him or hearing him confused her terribly and this evening she wanted to breathe correctly and calm her aching body. She felt ill because of him.

'And I can hear sirens.'

As the morning wore on, it became apparent that Harriet wouldn't be well enough for the Boxing Day Hunt later that afternoon. She looked pale and kept disappearing to the bathroom, which was most unusual for her and caused everyone else to comment.

'Harriet, whatever is the matter with you'?

'I'm fine Charity, honestly it will pass.'

But it didn't seem to pass, and it was Grace who confirmed her fate that afternoon.

'You are obviously sick dear, maybe all the rich food from the past few days has upset you.'

'For such a robust looking girl you are very sensitive dear' joined in Charity.

'Most surprising.'

'Grace, Charity please I want to come to the dance, I want some excitement this holiday.'

At her persistence Grace became more and more insistent and ignored her protestations.

'I have decided dear. You have germs and you will go to bed after a light lunch and sleep until you have rid yourself of this new poison.'

'Oh, for heaven's sake, I'm fine. Guy, what do you think? Please let me come, I'll be very well-behaved, and I promise not to dance if I feel at all queasy.'

He took one glance at his sister's pleading eyes and at once the answer was clear to Guy.

'Sorry Harry, I think your sisters are right, a day in bed will sort you out, don't you worry, besides we have to make you well for the New Year Celebrations, there are going to be fireworks and a band at the bandstand.'

'Please Guy, let me just try.'

'Come now little bird and give me a hug, I think you should go straight up to bed this instant, maybe lunch isn't the best idea after all. Come on now, off to bed.'

And with that a sulky Harriet, slouched out of the room, slamming the door as she went.

'Keep an eye on her Greta, would you.'

'Yes of course I will.'

Dammit thought Greta, there goes my relaxing afternoon and evening alone, how I need it! Still at least it was Harriet, who would be undemanding, and she loved her little friend, so it would be OK. She was quite sure on looking at her that she would soon be asleep anyway and she would then be left alone entirely with her muddle of thoughts.

'Through the quicksand we must go.'

Once in her room, Harriet buried her head in her pillow and let herself finally give in and she let out the most enormous laugh.

'Easy peasy lemon squeezy.'

'I am so very proud.' Said the picture of Mother on her bedside table.

She decided on what clothes she would wear quietly in her room, so that the others wouldn't hear her moving around above their heads. Although the twins were so looking forward to the hunt, she suspected she was the least of their concerns.

They had blood and fear and death for their afternoon's entertainment after all. It was simple to decide what to wear, it would be dear dead Dad's waistcoat which had worked so beautifully last time. Yes, she would definitely wear it tonight when she met the gang at the clock tower. She smiled to herself in remembrance of that special night, an awakening that had taken the group to a whole different level. It made her tingle and she felt warm and ready.

She lifted up her nightdress and looked at her naked body in the mirror, just the thought of Tustin's hand on her breasts made her nipples erect and she clasped her chest trying to imagine it was him. She went back into her bed and put the pillow between her legs and pushed against it enjoying the sensation. Not long to go and best of all no one would know.

At about 2pm she heard them getting ready to leave, Guy in a last minute panic over where he had put his riding gloves. She felt sure he would take the hip flask with some French brandy in it with him today, to help squash the social anxiety he so often felt in these situations. Knowing he had been so much better these last few months and they had not performed their usual daily routine except for a handful of times, Harriet hoped he would struggle through.

The clocks still ticked.

During these less frequent times Guy hadn't called out as much to the ghosts in the room, and she hadn't seen the tears. He had merely closed his eyes and slept with a smile on his face, and she knew he was back with Cheri and Unity in France, back in the sunshine. The eternal sunshine of the longing mind.

They had not had any particular statement or conversation about the ceasing of the ceremony, just a tacit understanding that this was to be the case and that he would call upon her when required now. He was sure he would always need it occasionally as he wasn't quite ready to let his beautiful wife and daughter out of his mind. A thorough cessation could make him loose his sanity and he still needed them.

If he could see them and could feel them, all from a little safe spoonful of medicine and brandy then of course he would still indulge.

Miraculous really.

Harriet couldn't help but think of her brother at the event today. He would be fine at the hunt as he liked to ride and there would be a lot of action and not so much talking. He would be able to gallop along with the others or ensure he became disentangled from the pack, so he could be alone and look out onto the wonderful countryside which always soothed.

Harriet knew he liked this, he once told her a story about how he'd sneaked off and ridden into the next field and stopped by the stream and let the horse enjoy a drink whilst he had a tipple from his hip flask. He told her how he saw the poor fox, who stopped to look at him startled. About to blow his whistle, as close as bringing the very thing up to his lips, he abruptly stopped as he saw the fear and the panting of the terrified animal and felt such empathy and kinship. So, he shooed him away in the opposite direction of the horses with their crusading and crushing hooves, deliberate and murderous in their task.

Deliberate and cold. And there was too much of that. Far too much.

Once he was back on his horse, he made sure he went to a field close to the hunt where he could hear the baying of the dogs and he blew very hard on his whistle. When they appeared in all their bloodthirsty glory, he pointed them in the wrong direction. They didn't get a fox that day. That night he had a glass of champagne at the reception ball and silently raised it to his friend the fox.

It was the ball that worried Harriet, the temptation of all the alcohol and nervousness of the occasion would result in him becoming incapable and melancholy and she would not be there to hold his hand and lead him to his bed. Would not be there to silently watch over him for a moment to settle him in his reverie. Nor would Greta's increasing influence and steadiness be there to soothe him or excite him either.

Stupid party, stupid people for not giving Greta a chance so they could see for themselves how utterly gorgeous she was. Guy would have taken her of course, insisted upon it even. She understood it had been Greta who had decided to not make it difficult for her brother and for that Harriet loved her a little bit more. It was a shame she would not be quite alone this evening and had a slight concern that darling Greta may take it upon herself to come and check on her, so she took it upon herself to see if she could create a person like shape in the bed and she'd just jolly well have to cross her fingers. It was lucky for the unknowing Harriet that Greta was so preoccupied.

'Does he want me? Am I in anyway lovable? He is not my husband. The blood spiralled in the fountain, upwards and upwards.'

'There was blood.'

Poor Guy would be left with the ice maidens at the ball, which for Harriet would have been a terrible prospect. At the hunt, the girls would undoubtedly be leading the pack, white ponytails swishing in rhythm with the horse's tail.

Swish, swash and tally ho.

Their beautiful derrieres would be sashaying and swaying in their anticipation of what was to surely come. They were a bit like Milly in that respect.

At the ball, Guy would have to accompany his beautiful sisters, put up with the stares and the whispers about how absolutely picture perfect they were.

Did he feel proud? Maybe just a little. But mostly it bored him.

He would have to mingle and indulge in small talk,

surely the hell of the middle classes and society. It was enough to turn anybody to drinking copious amounts of alcohol, anything to numb the torture. Harriet hoped very much, he would be sat next to a quiet unassuming sort at the meal, at least that would ease things somewhat for him.

Hearing a noise now on the stairs she quickly applied some more of the white powder she'd been putting on all day. It was so easy to make herself look pale and queasy. It made her think that she really should use this particular trick more often. Quickly jumping under the covers as just on cue she heard a knock at her door.

'Come in' she said wanly in her quietest voice.

'We are leaving now dear, give me your wrist. Your pulse is racing Harriet and I insist you stay in this bed for the rest of the day.'

At that the twins left, their eyes sparkling in delight at the upcoming hunt.

'We'll deal with that fox too, make Mother proud'

A moment later it was Guy who knocked on her door:

'Now be sure to let Greta know if there is any worsening and she will call me and the doctor. I'll come home straight away, I do hate to leave you old girl.'

'Really Guy, I'll be fine, I just need to be left alone tonight to sleep, please don't trouble Greta to check on me.'

'Ok, just rest now little one.'

'My dear little bird.'

Alone downstairs in the big house with the green front door felt rather liberating for Greta. She began her day alone by putting the kettle onto boil and placing two custard creams on a plate that wasn't duck egg blue.

She would ease into her thoughts and make the most of the silence. All was quiet upstairs, the poor dear must be asleep thought Greta, plenty of time for me to check on her later.

Greta took her tea in the front room and looked out onto the street in front of her, mistress of the house for once, surveying her realm with pride. Soon, she was lost in her thoughts, oblivious to anything except Guy, Henrich and the grandfather clock in the hallway ticking and tocking so very loudly.

Upstairs Harriet was eating her stolen bounty from the kitchen yesterday, some cuts of ham, a lump of cheese and hunk of bread, perfect. It would be enough to sustain her for the night's activities. They were meeting earlier today at 8pm as the nights were drawing in and she hoped to manage a few hours with her friends before they returned from the ball.

At the hunt the twins were the centre of attention, they were always admired by the men folk. Their jodhpurs pulled tightly, the mesmeric way they branded their crop, the stern way they spoke to their mounts. All tied together with their angelic faces, perfect in every way. Even better with a flick of mud or smear of blood.

'Bloody marvellous.'

'What gals.'

'Imagine, oh god, just imagine.'

Guy tried his best to be entertaining and witty, but found he lacked the competitive edge which most of his contemporaries seemed to so much enjoy. He was delighted to take a back seat to his sisters and it was easy for him to do his usual trick of absconding as soon as he could, by letting the pack stride ahead whilst he dawdled.

It was a beautiful clear blue sky, a crisp and fresh day and for a moment he was transported back to his French island.

He saw Unity run across the field in front of him.

'My little twinkling star.'

It was fleeting. Soon she had hidden behind the trees. He followed her of course, searching in the general direction.

'Baby girl, don't be cruel, come to me.'

'Unity, Unity dear.'

The sun passed away behind a cloud and he came back to the field in Warwickshire, alone with his horse for company.

'Unity, darling girl, Daddy's here!'

It had alarmed him at first, his visitations. But now he looked forward to them. He was especially delighted today because usually he saw them after the special medicine or after some drinks. Always at the house too, he'd never seen either of them out and about, not before today.

'Ahh my darlings, how I love you.'

'Thank you for visiting me this afternoon.'

He said it into the trees, into the wind and up into the beautiful blue sky.

It steadied him, he loved the countryside. He must have passed that down to his child, she obviously enjoyed it too. He was especially pleased she had come to Warwickshire, had seen where her forebears were from; danced in the same air as her father.

Spin.

Harriet heard movement outside her door and heard the knock, so she could prepare her face and wipe away any crumbs that were on the bed.

'Hello my little sparrow can I get you something to eat?'

Harriet ignored the question feigning sleep.

'Little one can you hear me?'

Again Harriet kept her silence, forcing Greta to come over and stroke her forehead.

'Greta is that you?'

'Yes my bird.'

'I've such a headache you know I think its best I stay in the dark and just sleep.'

'Ok my child if that is what you think best, but I will

check on you later.'

'Please don't Greta, I think its best I'm undisturbed so I can just sleep through, I'm so restless the slightest sound seems to trouble my head.'

At this, Greta kissed her damp forehead, cleverly dampened in water before she came in and whispered.

'Sleep my dear, let the fairies take care of you tonight my love.'

Once she was back downstairs, Greta admonished herself for taking pleasure in the fact that Harriet needed to be left alone. It was exactly what she had been looking forward to herself and as long as she was in the house that should be enough. The child wasn't too hot to the touch and she would call her if she needed her.

She fed Milly who was also delighting in the absence of the twins, the place felt a little freer, a little less threatening. There was no one here that would give her a little kick or hiss. Feeling emboldened, after her food she lay in prominent position on the sofa, stretched out and purring, which made Greta giggle.

'Ahh Milly, look at us, queens of the castle.'

'Maybe one day.'

She took a photograph of Guy in her hands and sat looking at it for some time before she fell into a much-needed deep sleep. The best place to solve life's problems.

At 7.50 precisely a much-improved Harriet tiptoed down the stairs. She was resplendent in her waistcoat and men's trousers, her black kohl eyes and lip glossed lips. Relieved beyond belief that Greta was dozing. Milly looked up as she passed the doorway and gave her a quizzical stare. Harriet placed her finger to her lip.

'Ssshhh'

'Hush little baby.'

At which, Milly rolled back over.

She lifted the latch and quietly closed it behind her,

feeling the cold air on her face and the rush of excitement spiked through her as she ran full pelt to the park gates. Checking no-one was looking, she then scaled them in her usual fashion. A coating of snow making it even more of a challenge which she was equal measure to.

The clock tower struck 8pm, which made the birds fly from their roof and Harriet took her cue to run for the door, they would soon all be together again.

CHAPTER 19

'Tustin?'

'Hilary, Jack?'

'Are you there?'

The door was open when pushed, so Harriet had assumed at least one of the others was inside. She hoped it was Tustin, who was the key holder after all. Smiling to herself, she thought they would have some moments together before the others arrived.

There was no sound from up above, just the ticking and the tocking of time's inevitability above her. How she wished she could stop it still every now and again. It would help to clarify her thoughts. But the world insisted on gambolling onwards into the unknown.

There was no light and it was much darker than their last visit. Away from the outside snow it was a cold and desolate dark place.

And there was a noise. A something.

'It's me, Harriet' she called upwards in a quiet voice.

'Come on down and give me a hand up, would you?'

She was met with silence. How peculiar. She heard the noise again. Whatever it was snuffled.

'Must be a fox', she said out loud to the walls to make it true.

Even so, it was enough to make her begin her climb up to the tower and with a little trepidation, she placed her foot on the first step.

'Get a ruddy grip Harriet!'

She told herself off for being such a scaredy cat, knew it was just the anticipation getting to her.

It was so dark, she didn't see the gap in the stairs and she missed her footing, causing her to stumble. She managed to hold on tight to the wooden rails at either side, but it ripped at her flesh and she could feel a warm drip running down her leg. It certainly hurt enough to be blood.

'Bugger.'

'Look, if anyone is already up there, I'm going to be simply furious.'

She steadied herself again and before long had made it into the room at the top of the tower. Something brushed past her foot and she heard scuttling.

'Oh no, not rats!'

Suddenly the room that had been a haven, that had caused them all such joy, felt like something else altogether.

Harriet felt thoroughly spooked now. How could she still smell candle smoke in the air? Her small pale hand stretched out to touch the candle, it was still warm.

'Tustin, come, on, joke over now.'

'Come out, please.'

Silence hang heavy in the air, the dead weight of it felt immense and her chest tightened and throat clenched in response.

'What was that?'

A definite snuffling, an animalistic breath came from somewhere at the back of the room. She turned slowly and deliberately as if in her turning it would somehow disappear and go away.

Facing her was a snarling set of teeth as scared as she and as she screamed it ran down the steps, light and quick on its feet and she heard it hitting against the door below.

'Bang, bang, bang, rhythmic in its desire to be free of the place, with each head butt the impact lessened as it became weary and desperate for escape, still it persisted.

It was her.

With trepidation she picked up the old broom and gingerly began to make her way downstairs.

She paused halfway down and saw the fox was dazed and exhausted now, a bloodied head and foaming mouth, it wildly turned and snapped at her, causing her to falter.

'Come along Harriet.'

Stern with herself now, she gained a little courage from the frightened animal below her, a soul even more scared than herself.

Reaching forward, she pushed at the door with the broom handle. It opened enough and soon the fox was out running as far away as possible from the tower and Harriet wasn't far behind.

Both bloodied and scared and surrounded by time.

Can you feel it baby?

Run!

She ran the few metres to the aviary at full pelt, her chest sore in the icy air and she gasped and faltered when she arrived at the safety of the iron roof.

The snow had begun to fall thick and fast. A wind from the northern lands of nowhere was churning up pockets of snow. The park was beautiful, but visibility low and she could only just make out the clock tower, so she decided she would wait it out with the birds until someone arrived.

Despite her blood pumping, she wished she had dressed in warmer clothes. This wasn't what she was expecting. This wasn't a short dash to the clock tower and warm hugs and eager hands, delighted at her arrival.

'Well birds, it's you and me, are you cold my darlings?'

The birds were quiet, they seemed oblivious to the gusts of wind, the dancing snow flurry.

The fury being whipped up.

That was outside and not yet inside.

Harriet crouched down, with her back to the cage looking outwards. The scene was mesmerising. Dancing fat snowflakes, swirling and gaining momentum, which couldn't quite reach her under the aviary roof, but clever little snowflake generals reached her boots, which she had to keep shaking off.

And there are always some things which you can't quite get shot of.

'C'est la vie ma petite.' said Mother.

She was there for some time, ages passed by, millenia stormed past, it all ticked by so very loudly in her head.

Time absorbed her and she was getting colder and colder, so cold it made her want to just rest her head and have a little sleep. Then she remembered Guy had told her about his time in France in the war and how that was the last thing she should do. So, she jumped up and stamped her feet, the birds behind her still quiet.

It didn't seem enough. It was time to embrace the snow.

A booted foot braved the outside, then a leg, and finally Harriet. She knew the stars were there above her head, she just couldn't see them.

Arms outstretched now, she dropped her hip and twirled.

Swaying in whiteness.

'Dance into oblivion my girls, there will be no finer way out.'

And so, shoulders shook, toes were pointed, head rolled. Hips swirled.

Silence, nothing, quiet, white all around.

Think. The park gates were in a line from the aviary. Pushing off theatrically from the colonnades of the bird house, she walked into the white.

...

'No!'

The hands grabbed her first before a face started to emerge from the nothing. They held her fast and soon she felt warm lips on hers, and the desire mixed with relief was too much for her. Soon her salty tears mixed with the kisses and she couldn't breathe and that was rather wonderful.

'I'll come to you,' said time.

'Harry!'

She was off her feet now and he was lifting her towards the clock tower. They made it as far as the stairs, before he placed a gloved hand under her trousers onto her bare thigh. She opened her coat and didn't mind exposing herself to the cold, to the blood on the floor, to her memory of the fox hitting his head on the door over and over again. That stench of animal blood, of a kindred spirit was still there. It mixed with her own now.

She felt his warmth, his excitement, his eagerness, her excitement and her eagerness.

'I've missed you.'

'Not here, not on the floor.'

He took her in his arms and before she knew it they were in the room, and the clock was ticking again and she was where she should have been over an hour ago.

There was a crash downstairs.

'What's all this blood?'

Jack. They heard him mount the stairs, enough time

for them to disentangle themselves. Harriet pulsed and felt overcome by the evening.

'Whatever's happened to you old girl?'

Jack took in the kohl smeared down her face, the bloodied hand, a cut lip from eager mouths. The shaking, the look of a night that had been spent.

Jack stole a hard look towards Tustin.

'It was so very cold Jack, there was a fox, no one was here, it was so dark,' gabbled Harriet

'Were you here earlier?'

'No of course not just arrived now, now come and have a hug, poor old thing.'

Five minutes later, Hilary arrived and Tustin had relaxed enough to be able to move and put his hand in his pocket and bring out the box. He'd tied it in a red ribbon, with a cheery label that read: 'for Christmas,' and placed it on the table.

Moments later, time which had seemed to be so important, had no relevance, no necessity and Harriet felt free. She felt no pain from earlier and she wasn't alone. She closed her eyes and the tune from Mummy's bedroom and Christmas day came back to her in waves and she felt the tears well up inside her again, but she didn't feel sad, it simply just was.

'It is, it is, it is.'

Morning came and no-one stirred. Greta wrapped up in confliction, Guy in visitation, Grace in chase, Charity felt the moon on her body and Harriet lived *that* song. Even Milly the cat, her fur as warm as a sun-drenched terracotta hilltop village was submerged in sleep.

The house took each small chance whenever it arose. It was bold this morning and began in full view by the fireplace in the sitting room. The place where the news of Henrich had been turned to ashes, where father's cigar ash had fallen, where mother had splashed her brandy to make the flames gallop and rise, where Greta had sobbed and the embers had spluttered to oblivion.

Its visibility was a risky calculation, it formed a perfect crack snaking around the mantel, at the end of which it allowed itself to expose the rust below and break out in a little pile of vibrant dust. They had moved things along a notch.

Someone decided on a walk later in the day. No-one noticed Harriet's hand, Harriet's pale and quiet or Guy's glassy eyes. They were all very much taken up with themselves. There was self-possession in the ether.

They walked up to Leicester Lane and took the turning to the big house with the tower room. It lay up a dirt track over farmland and took you past the walls of the house. It was favoured by dog owners of the new houses that were just going up in Kinross Road.

They all felt their lungs splutter a little as they rose higher. They turned and admired the view of the town, in its coat of snowy white.

The tower room of the house reminded Harriet of the clock tower and she felt a little uneasy as if her family could see Tustin's hands on her legs, on her stomach. She felt his hands cover her and she shifted, unsettled.

Exposed.

CHAPTER 20

The following morning was far removed from the previous day. Great wheels were turning as the house was prepared for their New Year's Eve entertainments. Greta didn't even notice the crack in the wall, it was hidden from view by a magnificent vase of oriental lilies, their scent intoxicating and all-encompassing in the room. The little pile of rust had been swept away and the slight musty smell hidden by the flowers.

'Harriet, I think you should wear the violet dress for our guests.'

'Charity, it's only us, Tustin and his aunt, the vicar and his wife, I'm sure no-one will care.'

'Honestly Harriet, we need to make Mummy proud don't we and don't forget some of the hunt crowd will be popping in.'

'Yes, Charity is right Harriet, we need to sparkle.'

'That's' what Mummy used to say Charity, don't be

such a copycat.'

Harriet was thrilled that Tustin would be there, the days since Boxing day had seemed intolerable and there was no way she would be wearing that dress tonight.

There had been blood, there had been tears, there had been dirt. Maybe she could be vibrant today.

Dazzle.

As they gathered in the hall before the hour of the party, Grace pinned a small flower on each of them. Guy breathed deeply and let it pass. If it made his sisters happy, for now he was prepared to wear the little violet. He did not wear his allegiance with pride unlike the others, he felt penned in by the pin, felt the metal lurch and stab its way down through his flesh into his organs, contaminating them. Lacerating his bond.

Still he took it graciously. He was good at that.

'Take it like a man.' Father spat.

The vicar arrived first. He was in his dress robes for the occasion, the purple loose fabric, hanging in folds that delighted the twins. The vicar unknowing what his choice of clothes meant was especially pleased at the response.

'Can we kiss you Vicar? It is New Year'

'Of course my child, it's a day to thank God and share his love for the coming year.'

'Vicar.'

'Ahh Harriet, Happy New Year.'

He looked upon her in great disappointment. With such charming and glorious sisters she really was the runt of the family, with her sullen air and the darkness that seemed to hang about her, wearing her in swathes.

'What a delightful home,' said the Vicars wife, the suitably named Celestine.

'I remember it from a party your mother held Guy dear, such a joy, such vibrancy, you must miss her terribly.'

'Yes of course, it was very sudden.'

She placed her hand on his cheek.

'Dear boy.'

Mother watched from her portrait.

'Mummy's darling.'

'Leave us Mother,' he whispered under his breath once he was alone and helped himself to a drink.

'Wearing violets for me, my pansy boy.'

Harriet made her way to the kitchen, slogging back the drink she had stolen from the party. If she was going to have to talk to these people all evening she best fortify herself. It would be such a bore until Tustin arrived.

'Such a difficult child,' said the Vicar, as he watched her leave the room.

'It would be easier for them if she wasn't here.'

'Come along George, don't be uncharitable, after everything that happened.'

'Celestine, you are a wonderful woman and I love you, but really.'

'George I won't tell you again, it happened here in this very house if you remember, it's no wonder the child is sullen.'

Then there were new voices and the house paused from its work under the floor.

'Celestine, George, you must remember Charlotte and Tustin. Rose's sister and boy.'

'Tustin, how you've grown, I remember last time I saw you, you were a little boy.'

'Haven't seen you in church recently.'

And at that Tustin made his excuses and left his aunt to field the vicar. She was so very bemused, she wouldn't mind at all. He couldn't see Harriet and he really wanted to. It was pressing. It was important. It was everything.

'Harry?'

'Harry, where are you?'

He made his way into the hallway, the ghastly picture of her mother staring out at him and he shivered. He used to hate the way she spoke to her, hated the way she used to kiss his cheek and hold him for a little too long smelling of alcohol. As he remembered he smelt her perfume, that sickly sweet violet smell, yuk. It turned his stomach.

'Still in position I see.'

He turned and made his way to the kitchen and tripped. As he did so, he thought he heard a giggle somewhere nearby.

Game on.

'Harry?'

She heard a noise in the hallway, wiped her mouth and quickly swilled with water from the kitchen tap and made her way outside.

'Tustin?'

'Come into the kitchen.'

Harriet pulled him towards her and they stumbled into the pantry, Harriet knocking a tin of custard as she went.

'Damn, don't let it get on my dress.'

'What are you doing in here, surprised the hawks let you out of sight.'

'Shhh, stop speaking.'

She pressed her body against his. He could feel each and every curve through the silk dress and she felt him harden.

'We didn't finish.'

'Harry, we can't, not with everyone in the house.'

He kissed her neck, the sensation made her wrap her thighs around him. He moved her onto a ledge and unclasped the top of her stockings.

'I don't see you complaining.'

She felt warm and wet and he enjoyed it as much as she did. His inexperience meant it was over quickly.

The house took to the pantry walls whilst they were preoccupied.

'Harriet?'

'Harriet, where are you? Come and join the party.'

Greta came into the kitchen and the pair froze, their breath on each other. It took every bit of reserve Tustin had to stay still, he could still feel her breasts under the silk.

'She's not in here Guy, would she have gone out into the garden for some air?'

When she had gone, Tustin moved away and got himself together.

'Don't go.'

'You're insane, we'll get caught and I'll never be able to come and see you, we've got to get back.'

'Spoil sport,' whispered Harriet.

'Ahh Tustin, there you are, have you seen our Harriet anywhere, the music is about to start and Guy would love her to be there.'

'Sorry Greta not in here.'

Harriet smoothed herself down, did up her stocking, took a swig of the cooking sherry and made her way back to the others.

'Harriet where have you been and what is that on your shoes?'

'I heard Milly in the kitchen Grace, she'd jumped on the ledge and knocked over the custard.'

'Oh, I'm so sorry everyone, I've no idea how she got in there, I was quite sure the door was shut.'

'Never mind Greta, let's not make the mistake next time, we can't afford to ruin another dress, now come along both of you, the music is about to start!'

Guy took his sister in, it was only a dusting of powder, honestly the twins could fuss rather. He looked across the room at Tustin and as he crossed his legs he saw the familiar yellow dust caught up in the bottom of his trousers.

'Come along Harriet, I've missed you dear sister, what can I do to keep you with me.'

And with that the music began and they began to dance, over and over again as if it were their last night on earth.

CHAPTER 21

They found her in the early hours of the morning. The park attendant had been alerted, after a nearby resident said the birds were making the most terrible racket.

'On New Year's Day', sighed a rather the worse for wear Sid. 'I was going to spend the day with the family.'

'I know but just check would you, shouldn't take you long, maybe a fox got close last night or something.'

'I'll just finish my tea then, can't be that urgent.'

Sid knew something remarkable had happened before he even got there. Over the years he had got used to the birds and could tell their mood by the sounds they made.

He couldn't quite explain this particular noise, the cacophony that hurt his ears and troubled his soul as he approached the aviary on that most awful of mornings.

Later that day, he tried to put it into words at the police station and the best he could come up with was 'frenzied', the birds sounded full of a frenzy, a dangerous, excited screech.

Sid told them he felt bad, he should have run on hearing the noise, but he didn't. He approached slowly instead, preparing himself with each step and steadying himself for whatever it was he would find.

It wasn't going to be good, that much he knew.

He didn't tell them he'd waited twenty minutes after the call to finish his breakfast. He couldn't even admit that to himself.

You don't just leave a boiled egg and soldiers.

Sid saw her wrist and hand first which had managed to fall through the netting. The woman's fingernails were full of blood and feathers as if she had been trying to tear her way free.

He felt the bile rise within his throat and it was with some trepidation that he forced his unwilling eyes to look at the full scene in front of him.

Her hair was matted with dried blood and she was covered with peck marks. The worst of it was where he could see where actual chunks of skin and flesh had been torn away. A piece of something human hung from her leg.

The body was lying on the ground surrounded by feathers and lay twisted and ugly in the morning light.

Sid was not equipped for anything like this. Sid had just eaten. Sid had been up all night celebrating. This was not how the beginning of a new year should start.

Her knee looked dislocated, the ankle was facing the wrong way, and she must have had a terrible fall. Perhaps the most alarming thing of all was her right eye which was bloodied and not in its rightful place, a piece of something hanging slightly out of the socket.

The birds quietened when he arrived and now left the body alone. He saw blood around the parrot's beak and he suspected that he was responsible for the larger wounds. This saddened Sid because he was a marvellous

152

creature really, magnificent in colour and voice. He had no idea they could be violent, he would be shot for sure now and he wasn't happy about it.

The other birds looked sated; they had, had their fill and weren't interested anymore. The day was getting on now, the light was rising and he needed to begin to clear up and alert people.

Trying not to look at the body, he cordoned away the birds as best he could. He thought he should do that first, in case they decided to attack him next.

At one point he realised he would have to move her leg with the tights ripped almost clean away. Very carefully he lifted it up. God she was just a girl, maybe not much older than his own daughter. A sob began somewhere far back in his throat and a few tears escaped and splashed on the bloodied leg, making it a pale pink liquid which ran gently, quietly away.

Sid was captivated by this for a moment and didn't hear the noise at first. It was very quiet, almost imperceptible. He thought it was the wind, maybe a squirrel or rat was running past. But then he heard it again, stronger this time.

Her mouth, that pretty young swollen mouth, which spoke of youth and promise, was moving. He looked at her eyes and saw all the fear and pain and life, life! My god she was alive.

'Mother?'

Sid worked quickly now and without hesitation. He steadied her head and gave her a sip of the fortified wine he always carried with him, since the war. It made her cough and splutter, but colour came to her wrecked pale body. Gently, he lay his coat over her, for the cold and for her modesty.

'Thank you.'

When he had steadied her and reassured her that the birds couldn't get to her, he ran full pelt, as best as his war gas damaged lungs would take him. He felt terribly guilty at leaving her and could tell it scared her, but he had no choice.

He reached the telephone box quickly and rang for the police and ambulance. In the box looking out onto the tranquillity of the park and the streets in their early morning glow, what he had just witnessed seemed impossible.

It was going to be a bright crisp sunny, beautiful winter's day. Sid watched the two herons, that liked to stand near the ornate fountains fly past, and he was struck by their beauty and grace. At the best of times he thought they looked otherworldly, but today even more so. It was a welcome moment of calm whilst he spoke of the terrible things he had seen.

Once he had finished, he ran back as quickly as he had travelled there. The only sound now being the blood rushing in his head.

The girl's breathing was very laboured and she was icy cold to the touch. Sid gently lifted her now onto his lap and they sat together in shock and silence, waiting. He took off his park attendant jacket and wrapped it over her, so she had two layers of warmth. His thin coat may not have been enough.

Help didn't take long, he heard the sirens and mentally tracked the sound to the park gates. He read the disbelief in their eyes. Sid told them he'd cleared it up a bit and made the birds safe. A stretcher bearer arrived shortly after the police and he lifted the girl out of the dirt to safety.

'Careful, now,' said Sid.

The girl was as precious to him as the crown jewels now.

She was given an injection of something, which he hoped would take her momentarily to a happier better place.

'Wouldn't mind a bit of that myself mate.'

Sid attempted a laugh, that just wouldn't come.

…

That was the last he saw of her for a very long time. Or so it seemed to Sid.

Once the police had finished with him, he went to the Warnford Hospital and sat and waited to hear of news.

He hated the hospital. It was a rather grand Victorian building which was imposing, and it smelt of bleach and pain. You could feel the suffering. It reminded Sid of bad times and yet still he waited, desperate to know how she was. He had been allowed to sit in her ward's waiting room, but not allowed in to actually see her.

'Family only, I'm afraid sir.'

He saw the famous Leighton twins go in and he assumed that the poor girl must be the younger sister. The brother came and he looked familiar too. His face was red and troubled, he obviously hadn't slept either. The girls looked as calm and glacial as ever. He was pleased for her that she had her family there.

After some hours, he was told that she was now stable and would be OK. On hearing that, this quiet man left and went home to his wife and slept for the rest of the day and night, exhausted and mentally worn out by the day's activities.

It was a moment that Sid would never forget.

They were told how very lucky to be alive she was, her injuries and the cold combined made her condition quite serious.

'Mother?'

Her first words to Guy were a surprise to all of them. She asked for her mother and said she was with her all the time in the aviary, or the cage as she called it. The doctors said it was the shock that made her say such things. That her poor mind was looking for comfort and her dead mother represented that.

The twins of course readily agreed to this theory, but it troubled Guy. Harriet was not known for trips of fancy and esoteric thought. Guy also doubted that his mother represented comfort, she certainly didn't to him, but just maybe she had been to Harriet, the youngest of the children. He had been in France after all for much of her upbringing and could have missed the strength of their feeling for one another.

'Up the wooden stairs to Bedfordshire.'

He knew that Harriet was also troubled by his mother's presence in the home, he saw how she looked at the painting in the hall as if it was alive and breathing. As if that cruel mouth was speaking to her.

'Sleep my dearest little one.'

Whilst Harriet slept that afternoon, he decided to pay a visit to the park and try and see for himself what on earth made her enter the aviary. What made her go to that place (and at night, a cold night) at all. He needed to try and make sense of it all somehow as no one had managed to offer him a reasonable explanation at all.

There had been music and dancing and sway and chatter and laughter.

They had gone to bed, hadn't they?

Now it was a quiet evening, as he walked up to the scene of the crime. The birds had been released back fully into the building and were sitting quite happily on their perches. There was no sign of a parrot however and Guy knew that he must have been removed permanently.

'Shoot the bastard.'

Harriet had spoken about the parrot in her hospital bed, she spoke of the colours of the wings. A vibrant cobalt blue, like the deepest pools in the sea and reds that reminded her of a dessert in a sunset, fully filling her eyes and senses.

'Belle, belle.'

How beautiful it was, she seemed to almost have forgotten how vicious also. Harriet seemed to smile and drift off when talking of the colours as if it was a beloved pet.

'Such beauty, such kindness.'

The blood had been scrubbed away, in fact the floor looked unnaturally white, the cleanest it had been in a long time. Guy thought that rather ironic and even in his upset it made him smile.

'Cleanliness is next to Godliness darlings.'

He stood for some time just watching the birds as they moved and ate and flew around inside the giant cage. They seemed so peaceful and at ease and after a while he actually found that it soothed him, and he became a little lost in it.

He threw a stick through the gap and it didn't trouble them at all. He rationalised that it wasn't the same as a person suddenly arriving in their home, but all the same he thought it odd that they had attacked her and so badly.

The sun started to go in and he found himself getting cold. The clock chimed, goodness had he really been here for that amount of time. He should get back to Harriet at the hospital, the twins would have been there for too long and he hoped to be there when she next woke up. It was important that it would be his face that she saw.

'I will always take care of you.'

It was just as he was leaving and a golden glow had surrounded the aviary, which made the white of the little dove's wings appear crystalline against the light, like tiny angels; that he saw a glimmer of purple in the corner. It must have previously been shielded by one of the birds. Or maybe it was the changing of the light and shadows which made him see it sitting there, but it was unmistakeable.

There lay a violet, crushed and trampled and dying in the corner.

He stared at it for a while, to make absolutely sure that his eyes weren't deceiving him and that it was definitely there. He made himself blink a few times and even walked away and came back, but it was undeniably there. It must be truth lying in the corner as he hadn't had his medication yet.

Spin and sink and sink and swim.

It made him feel a bit shaky, made his legs weak at the knees and his head felt dizzy and he thought he might faint. He knew he must leave the spot, but he was finding it hard to move. His legs and his eyes were just captivated on the floor and its most horrible purple stain.

'Clean everything up now, my little love.'

A bird jumped on the screen in front of his face and it jolted him into moving, which at last took his eyes away from it. As he walked through the park and over the suspension bridge on his way back to the hospital he paused on the bridge and watched the water furiously gushing beneath him. It gave him some clarity.

Just maybe, Harriet hadn't been lying when she said that Mother was with her in the cage. Just maybe it wasn't a hope of security, and she didn't dream it up for a comfort.

Just as the parrot's wings were the red of the dessert, Mother had been with her last night. It had been the truth and this thought carried him as quickly as he could back to her bedside.

'Mummy won't ever leave you darlings.'

'I made you.'

CHAPTER 22

The house seemed cold and unwelcoming without Harriet, Greta missed her dreadfully. It was as if the soul of the building had gone away. Milly too seemed at odds and Greta was finding it difficult to find any food that she would take to. She had even started to warm her chunks up a little, as if the smell would help her work up an appetite. She slept a lot, as did Greta, lying up on her bed not sure what to do after her chores.

Guy was pre-occupied and seemingly uninterested.

She understood, as always.

Harriet was his special little star and the beginning and end of his small real world. It was just how it was.

He kept himself to himself a lot at the moment and she had started to find those sticky sweet brandy stains on the floor in the front room. The room he used to spend all that time with Harriet in. It was beginning again.

Slither and zither.

The building felt it, its chilly walls grew a little colder and a little damper and decided to go wild, with cracks appearing here and there and everywhere. The pantry was now almost unusable. The wall that had seen her stockinged legs, had seen her breasts, had felt her tears splash against its surface, the walls that knew her secrets.

No one cared about it or commented on it.

Absorbed.

It was nice to see Guy on occasion, even if he was somewhere else in his head. His apparent nonchalance for her, made the affection she had for him grow a little more each day. It was his pain which made her want to comfort him. More and more layers of pain. It was intoxicating.

The guilt she felt about all of it added to the intensity.

He had touched her shoulder this morning as she was making breakfast and it made her flutter inside.

'Drop kick darlings.'

She was experienced enough to know that this meant that she undoubtedly and absolutely loved him. She didn't want to upset her dead husband, didn't want to feel like she was betraying him, didn't want, didn't want.

Couldn't stop, couldn't stop.

Perhaps when they were all past this difficult spell and Harriet was home, he would embrace this love, this whatever it was.

It would all come out into the open at some point. Everything always did. Greta was surprised at how much she relished that moment. She was unused to big and high-water feelings. Had she really been coasting for all of this time?

She felt emboldened and guilty and weak as a kitten, all at the same time. There was insanity and she was a part of it all now.

Without Harriet and a sense of balance and basic nurturing that they all indulged in, there was little to stop the family divide. There were now definite factions within the house, the twins and the two of them on opposite sides. Even if Guy didn't want her, that was where Greta most certainly hoisted her petard.

In between hospital visits, the girls were in a 'creative' phase, which meant that they kept themselves locked away for most of the time. Sketches were found in the bins, torn up and crossed out. They seemed lost in their thoughts a lot and were only really heard in the evenings. They had stopped getting up for breakfast and would sleep through in their pristine rooms. The sunlight streaming in never seemed to bother them, they kept their curtains wide open and embraced it.

As Grace said to Guy 'We need the light so much dear brother, the dark is upon us again.'

And Mother was uncharacteristically silent from the painting in the hall.

Greta went in on one of the first mornings after the incident to check they were OK. She went to Charity's room first and was blinded by the white. White head against white sheet, white light bouncing of white furniture, it was dazzling. There wasn't even the faintest blush on her cheeks. Greta wished she had a way of capturing this odd and unsettling scene. She was truly beautiful and otherworldly.

The picture was repeated in Grace's room, she looked as serene as her sister. Calm, tranquil and utterly at peace. She stood in the doorway for some time just watching her. It made her feel drab and unlovely. They were extraordinary.

There were no churned up blankets tossed aside, sheets doused in sweat. Hot and peculiar even in January. They weren't like Greta. They slept like the grave, it was beyond cold it was immense.

For all of it, they were something else.

CHAPTER 23

The third sister who had, had something else happen to her was physically making good progress. There was talk of moving her to convalesce somewhere 'quiet and distant.' The distant part bothered Guy.

'How can I watch over her if she's somewhere I'm not.'

The twins seemed happy with the arrangement and with Uncle William arranged a stay at a home in the lakes.

'They deal with trauma Guy, it's on the lake, it will do her good.'

And with that it was a done deal and the twins returned to an intense creative phase, paintings were strewn everywhere. Both Greta and Guy assumed this distant, creative phase was because they were dealing with what had happened to Harriet in their own way, although when they did see them, they seemed quite cheerful, if a little business like.

'Darling, we are in the zone.'

Slither and zither.

Guy had tried to talk to Grace yesterday evening. She didn't seem to mind at all anymore about Harriet not being in the house, in fact she said how 'homely' everything felt and how 'nice' and 'right' the place felt. She had even kissed Guy on the cheek and told him not to worry.

The following week, a telegram arrived from Uncle William addressed to Guy. Charity and Grace had intercepted its arrival and now followed Guy into the library to watch him read it. Uncle William wrote about a brilliant new business opportunity that he wanted to include Guy on which would secure the girls future if it pulled off. It was apparently, 'too good an opportunity to be missed,' and he hoped that Guy would come and meet with him to discuss it further. It would mean him going to visit Uncle William for a few weeks to secure the deal.

On reading it, Guy's initial thought was to turn the offer down, much as it sounded very good, he didn't want to leave the family at this moment, especially after what had gone on. He still felt terrible about his abandonment of his sisters after the war and now felt more than ever such a strong sense of duty to stay and try and help things get back to normal, whatever that meant with this family. If he was really honest with himself as well, he didn't want to leave Greta. He found her a comfort.

How peculiar that was.

Perhaps it was just the game. An easy game at that.

The twins however were very keen for him to go, insistent even. They told him, that Harriet in her convalescent home in Windermere would be close by, he could stop off on his way up and even spend the weekends with her, whilst he was there, it wouldn't be far from his meeting in Haugh of Urr. It would do them both the world of good. Charity said it would give her peace of mind, to know that they were at least together. Terrible really, that at the moment it was simply impossible for them to travel that far.

'We need to give into our calling Guy.'

'We are…bidden.'

Guy may have doubted Charity's words of sympathy, but it was undeniable that it was a strong argument for him to take Uncle William up on his offer.

'I'll think it over this evening girls.' Despite him already knowing in his heart that he would of course be making the trip. It was too irresistible not to see her.

The icing on the cake, came when Grace asked him if the money would help with Harriet's medical bills, should she need any ongoing care. That the mind can be a tricky beast to control and it would be helpful if they had some reserves.

'The money will be so helpful brother, our recent paintings weren't as well received as we all hoped, fashion is a terribly precarious thing.'

'Despite us being timeless Charity, classic and elegant. The masses are such fools at times, but there we are. At the moment we are both 'out' as opposed to 'in'.'

'Quel dommage.'

'We are slaves, dear brother, slaves to creation. We need to work.'

Guy found Greta in the garden with the cat. She was dragging a stick along the floor and Milly was playfully chasing it. He sat her down and placed her hand in his lap. She knew what was coming, she'd seen the telegram, she'd read it where it was left on the table, when she was cleaning.

'I know.'

'I have to go Greta, I'm so sorry, it won't be for long, I'll be back, and I hope I'll be able to bring Harriet back with me.'

He squeezed her hand and she looked at him with a

longing she didn't hide very well. She stood before he could kiss her and walked quickly inside.

Guy stayed in the garden a while.

Strangely compelling being wanted.

He thought of his wife on the beach at the island, her hair clinging to her neck as she appeared from under the waves. The curve of her waist, the line of those hips and the small breasts walking towards him as he lay watching and waiting on the warm sand. He felt her kiss him, her hair dropping tiny droplets of water onto his warm body. The tingle, oh the tingle! Her laughter, the taste of the salt. Him inside her there on the sand, the light so bright, the sun burning his naked body.

He had, had his moment it would seem. Or had he? He smiled.

There was a flurry of activity the next morning. The twins woke early for the first time in a number of weeks and were instructing Greta in the kitchen.

'He'll need food for the journey, perhaps a sandwich or something dear, we can't have him reliant on the London, Midland and Scottish Railway, now can we.'

Charity even ironed a fresh shirt for him to wear, 'he must look his best.' She also produced an envelope of pictures for Harriet, 'to cheer her up' and placed them in the top of his day bag. 'So, the dear girl knows how much she is still in our thoughts'.

Greta made herself scarce as Guy was about to leave, she didn't want a repeat of what had happened in the garden. He knew how she felt and that was enough. Guy spent his last hour looking for her, wanting to say goodbye and apologise. Had he embarrassed her? This turn of events was surprisingly irresistible. Maybe Mother had taught him something of use after all.

'Distant and dear, darlings. The combination that will finally make them succumb.'

'Ahh my beautiful ones, the choice will be yours.'

'Yes Mother.'

'Quite the bore, but if you feel an iota then it can be thrilling.'

'Putty in your beautiful hands.'

She wasn't wrong.

The twins cheerfully waved him away and made sure that he promised to telegram them with news of Harriet and of course about the business opportunity. They both kissed their brother goodbye and closed the door.

'We have two weeks at best.'

'It's enough time.'

'We can all be together again, how it should be.'

Charity ran up the stairs singing her favourite tune, Grace giggled as she locked the door.

Greta could feel a difference in the house, even though they were a few people less, it seemed cloying and claustrophobic. The revolution was almost automatic, it made her feel dizzy. She couldn't pinpoint what it was exactly, and she wondered if maybe she was getting under the weather. Maybe a chill was slowly starting to take hold. She certainly felt cold, icy even.

The twins spent the remainder of the day upstairs and Greta stayed with the cat in the kitchen cooking to give herself a sense of purpose, a grounding and to make the space feel more normal, whatever that was.

The girls didn't even appear for dinner that evening. Greta went looking for them and she received a dismissive; 'not today Greta, we need to watch our figures', in reply from Charity. Grace added more cheerfully. 'In fact don't worry about food for the next few days, it will be a nice surprise for when Guy and Harriet return, we will be as trim and supple as runner beans!'

And so, Greta and the cat shared a piece of fish and bread and butter and decided to call it an early night.

In her room that evening, Greta felt a pain in her

chest. Maybe the fish had disagreed with her. It felt incredibly intense and seemed to swallow her up. She felt pinned to her chair, couldn't move, and couldn't even call out, although to whom she didn't know. The cat sat staring at her with her head on one side in confusion. Some minutes passed, and the cat started to nudge at her, and when that didn't work, nibble at her fingers to get a response.

'Henrich, is this the time?'

Eventually she slept in the same spasmed position with the cat curled up at her feet. Milly sensing that if she lay close enough, she would ensure that she stayed alive. She had strange dreams, could hear the children's mother and thought she could hear movement downstairs. She was stiff when she eventually managed to move, the pain was a little better but still there and for the first time since Henrich had died, she cried. She cried for a long time, great gulping sobs that just wouldn't stop.

Afterwards the pain subsided but she felt wrung out, exhausted, sated of all emotion. She decided as she didn't have to cook for the girls, wouldn't even see them probably, that today she would stay in her bed and whatever it was that was troubling her would ease. She wasn't even sure if it was her body or mind that was causing such pain.

It couldn't be that Guy had gone could it? The heartache could not be so instantaneous surely. Was it Henrich? Oh, how she missed his calming presence. 'Get a grip,' she shouted at the room, she must just be overtired with all the events that had happened recently, overwrought and exhausted. That would be it.

She let the cat out of the room, with every intention to let it back in after she had, had a good rest.

Downstairs in the white house, whilst she slept it was a hive of activity, pictures were being placed on every single wall and flowers were placed in vases they didn't even know that they had. The twins sang and readied and busied the house whilst they could. The mould began its journey once more, no longer petrified. Cracks appeared within cracks.

CHAPTER 24

Guy reached the Lake District in the early afternoon, he was tired, but wanted to see Harriet as soon as he could, so he didn't stop off at the hotel at first, he took a taxi straight to the home.

The house was in a beautiful spot, sitting on the banks of Lake Windermere, with wonderful views down the lake and it lifted his spirits no end to think of Harriet in this place.

He was met by a kindly doctor who took him outside into the cold icy January air to see his sister, bundled up against the cold under a pile of blankets. She was staring into the water at a fixed spot and seemed to be muttering something that he couldn't quite understand.

'Still, we are used to little quirks,' he said to the outside.

Her right eye was still bandaged up and he was surprised at her thinness, not just from the slow walk back to health, but her whole demeanour was one of fragility and smallness and fear. Harriet had the same look about her as Cheri had just before the end.

'Harry darling.'

'Harry, it's me, Guy.'

She turned to face him after some moments but didn't stop muttering whatever it was into the air to be carried across the lake and down to the icy depths.

'What did you do?'

'What did you do?'

'What did you do?'

'Harry, it's me, what do you mean darling girl?'

'What did you do?'

And with that she turned her head from him and looked back over the water, hoping the wind and the waves would carry her message.

He pulled up a chair next to her, and she flinched when he tried to take her hand, and so he just sat there next to her for a while in silence.

And then she appeared, out there on the water which he knew was impossible. He looked at his sister, who was repeating the same words over and over.

'What did you do?'

She must be standing on a rock which he couldn't see, submerged under the water, it was the only explanation. There was his darling girl looking straight at them. Unity lifted her hand and began to wave, slowly at first, then more frantically as if something was urgent. The smile had gone from that little perfect face and concern had taken its place.

'Unity, Daddy is here.'

Harriet turned to look at him and took his hand for the first time in the minutes that had passed. She gripped it hard, digging her nails into him. He was transfixed though now on the water.

'What did you do?'

'What did you do?'

She dug her fingernails harder into his hand and could see the redness spring up in little pools under them.

Still he didn't flinch, still focussed on that sweet little

face.

'What's troubling you ma petite?'

'Daddy's here.'

'What did you do?'

Then Harriet did another extraordinary thing, in a month of extraordinary things. She followed his eye line and looked into the water, then she stood up still grasping her brother's hand.

'What did *he* do?' Eyes straight ahead.

Harriet let go of his freshly bloodied hand now and walked towards the water's edge, a trail of blankets in her wake. She stumbled a few times as they got entangled in her feet.

But she wasn't far away now, just a few steps and she would be in the water, would be able to grasp at that little hand and bring her to the shore.

'Miss Leighton?'

'Harriet!'

Turning, she saw them coming towards her now, running from the house. She didn't have much time, seconds even, so she jumped.

The cold water took her breath away and she felt herself fall a little, already she couldn't touch the bottom.

'Spin and twist and twist and spin girls.'

On hearing her mother's voice in her head, she managed to recover herself. Harriet could still see her, although she was further out than she looked, each time she thought she could stretch out and grab her, the child seemed to move away, out of her grasp.

Harriet swam on. She could feel them in the water now, heard the splash and the lake started to be disturbed, creating more and ever more ripples, making it harder to make quick progress.

'Harriet, Harry darling, my little chickadee.'

It was her brother calling her now, it startled her, and

she heard it above everything else. Suddenly it became very difficult to move, to breathe and she felt very, very cold.

As Harriet slowed, the child reached out to her. The little one had stopped waving and was smiling at her, just the sweetest smile. Harriet slipped under the water where it was dark and murky and peaceful, and in a brief moment wondered whether to look at the sky again. Here she was enveloped in an unknown darkness that didn't scare her.

'Go!'

She heard the little one's voice, she must be very close by now, the current must have carried her close by.

'One more push Harriet Leighton,' she told herself, and with that she launched her cold and aching body out of the water, hands outstretched, but she grabbed at the air, the cold and icy air and the little girl had gone.

'Harriet!' The voices were more urgent now.

She floated. Her body weak and tired, it would soon all be over, and she found that she didn't mind, not one jot.

Hands on her, always on her, dragging and pulling. Her head hurt. The lawn, the sky, the piercing blue of a winter's day, the light was too bright she wanted to be safe in the murk. There was blood on her feet, always blood, always there.

'Perhaps you should have some sugar sir?'

Guy was in the lounge of the house by the lake, a fire had been lit, he had been brought tea and they had found him a gown to wear. His shoes and socks had got a little wet as he had stood ankle deep in the water watching his girls. He hadn't been silly and dived in.

As he gazed into the fire and sipped his sugary tea, he felt his spirits lift immensely. It would all be OK he told himself, and he was so pleased that the girls had finally met. Unity had finally seen her auntie. Of course they weren't that far away in years, and it had delighted him to see them together. Yes, it was a tad chilly outside and he knew that the cold water would have been a shock to Harriet. She wasn't used to the water unlike Unity, who'd spent most of her life splashing around in the shallows. He smiled. They looked like they were playing such a game.

'The doctor suggests a brandy Mr Leighton.'

The same kindly nurse now proffered him a glass, ahh brandy. He suspected it wasn't French, but it was a good substitute and tasted enough like the good stuff to really enhance his mood.

The song came to him and he sat quite contentedly humming quietly to himself, warm and enveloped by the taste.

'Mr Leighton.' It was dark outside now and the fire was still cheerfully burning in its grate. He must have drifted off.

'What time is it?'

'Seven thirty sir, you have been asleep for a few hours.'

'Would you come and have a few words with the doctor please.'

'Yes of course, I'll follow you.'

He was waiting for Guy in his study. Forest green walls, an old leather chair on coasters that span if the mood took you. A solid rose oak desk with papers strewn, a clock sombrely marking the passing of time. Books covered one side of the wall, leather bound for the most part and in the bay window a man in a dark suit and blue bow tie.

'One doesn't often see one of those these days.'

'Mr Leighton?'

'Bow tie, top notch.'

'Take a seat.'

'Your sister is making good progress after the day's activities, we think a little hypothermic, but we are monitoring her and her fever has at last broken.'

'Thank goodness Doctor, I know she is in safe hands.'

'I must ask Mr Leighton, what prompted her to take to the water, did you not think it wise to stop her sooner?'

'Why no old chap, I just thought she was taking a stroll to the water's edge. We don't have lakes or sea in Leamington Spa, they are a novelty to us I think.'

'I see.'

Guy stood up and walked to the window.

'It's so very beautiful here, it will do her good.'

'You must be aware Mr Leighton that your sister requires a high level of care at the moment and is very ill, we must try and make her tremors and nightmares go. You do understand?'

'Yes of course, I myself had a little episode, the war you know, but we Leighton's are made of sterner stuff.'

'Your hand Mr Leighton, have you hurt yourself?'

'Oh that, it's nothing, can I see her?'

'Come back in the morning, she needs to rest undisturbed, she could have died today.'

He marvelled at the brother of the psychotic traumatised girl, such gung ho spirit, typical of those who fought for the country. He had some more questions, but they could wait.

CHAPTER 25

In his hotel that evening after a hearty stew and burgundy, well he was celebrating the girls meeting, he took to his bed and slept straight through. No dreams, no worries, he slept like the dead and awoke refreshed and ready for the day. He was a man invigorated.

He had postponed his meeting and had told uncle William about the little swim Harriet had taken. Naturally he had omitted the information that so easily troubled others, they could all be so sensitive at times. Before long a taxi had arrived to carry him on his way to the lake house.

'Can I see my sister today?'

'Not quite yet Mr Leighton, the doctor would like to ask some more questions, could you possibly wait a while? I could make you some tea.'

'Yes of course, anything to check the old girl is OK, I'll take my tea on the lawn if that is agreeable?'

From the forest green walled room, the doctor stood in his bay window and observed the brother, taking up position down by the water's edge. He watched him drag a chair all the way down, as near as he could be before he was on the incline. Serena followed with a blanket and he saw them laughing, a little flirtation perhaps. She was still smiling when she reached the house.

'Unity, I'm alone now, come along dear, come and see Daddy.'

Curious, thought the doctor, how he seems to want to be so close to yesterday's shocking scene. Perhaps he was trying to empathise with his poor sister, he would ask him later.

He saw Serena return and give him a mug of tea, she lingered a while and once again the pair seemed to enjoy a laugh before she came back to the house. It pleased him that the event hadn't worried him too much. He sometimes found that some relations after a drama, liked to keep their distance. This obviously wasn't the case with this family and that gladdened him.

'Unity come here.'

'Now, child, come now.'

His voice had turned a little stern, why did she not visit him today? The setting was perfect. The sun was shining again, the water calm and yet nothing.

Harriet watched from her upstairs bedroom, blank and dead to all of it.

The doctor saw him gesticulate into the air, pointing, seemingly frustrated, angry maybe. It seemed to make sense, of course he was cross after what had happened, and this was his release. He span around in his chair, as was his want, and returned to his notes, he would call for him when he was finished.

Later back in the study which was lined with books, the doctor spoke to Guy.

'She has had a good night considering, we gave her a little opiate to calm her, but don't be alarmed, we needed her to sleep well, often the best remedy don't you think so?'

'Of course doctor, I believe that opiates have their place and this was such a moment, thank you. I myself have had occasion to use them and know how healing they can be.'

'Really Mr Leighton, how interesting.'

'Medically prescribed of course, I think we all needed a little help after the war, you know.'

'Quite right, but you don't indulge any more of course?'

'What need is there when one can have a decent bottle of wine occasionally!'

'Quite. Now Harriet I'm afraid has suffered an episode, we are hoping that we won't have to turn to electroconvulsive therapy, but we must of course keep that as an option.'

'Did she say anything that may have resulted in yesterday's 'emotion?'

'No doctor, in fact we were simply marvelling at the water, quite a magnificent view.'

'Well in that case, we can hope that what happened was a misguided rush of enthusiasm, youthful delight at her surroundings, maybe having you there gave her some confidence, and she felt she could take to the water. I was of course worried that it was a traumatic response and she was reminded on seeing you of the incident with the birds?'

'I will say that we will be closely monitoring her mood and her health over the next few days, the water is so terribly cold at this time of the year, it's easy to get a chill and we don't want it on her lungs of course.'

'Of course doctor, whatever you see fit, I can see her before I go?' And with that Guy stood up expecting to be led to his sister. He so wanted to talk about his beautiful daughter with her, she would really understand now.

'Ahh, I'm afraid not at this moment Mr Leighton, please sit back down'

'But I insist!'

'It's a little delicate but considering her condition and

the positive effect you have on her, I think as her doctor, she is best left undisturbed, who knows what new confidence will spring itself upon her.'

'But…'

'I have explained it to her myself this morning and she accepts and wishes to give herself the best chance of recovery.'

'But I'm her guardian, I must insist.'

'Your concern is admirable Mr Leighton. Let us compromise, come and see us again on your way back from your meeting, she will be more stable by then, it will only be a week or so, give her more time.'

With no outlet for his anger, Guy walked or rather marched away from the place that housed his sister. Was she so selfish, to have stolen Unity from him? Well he may give her this week, but he would return.

It was dark by the time he got back to the hotel. The walk had taken him a few hours and he could add exhaustion on top of his disagreeable emotions.

The maid brought him up some hot water in a jug. As she was pouring it into the basin for him, he took her waist. He surprised himself and his utter unquenchable need to punish himself and all of them. There was no resistance, she was pliable and willing, a warm large girl with layers of flesh that wobbled and quivered and devoured his thin hands.

'Why Mr Leighton, I said you were a dark horse.'

He thrust into her with some force, grasping at her flesh which spilled out between his fingers. She wasn't alarmed, in fact she expected more and more from him, and when she later sat on him he felt that he would suffocate. But still he let her, and he put his head in between those heaving breasts and came loudly screaming her name.

'Mother.'

Afterwards, she got up and took her reddened

scratched nakedness to the basin and he watched her washing herself down with his flannel. He saw how the heat affected her pale flesh and it faintly disgusted him. It wasn't his wife, who was so different, with her slim taut tanned frame and not how he imagined Greta to look naked. Ah, Greta, so far away and so surprisingly intriguing.

As he went downstairs they all smiled at him, had the girl told them, had they heard? He didn't think he cared, he was the war veteran visiting his sick sister after all. An absolute bloody hero.

The taxi to the station took him past the lake house but there was no sign of either of his girls, so he continued his journey northwards.

'It is, it is, it is,' said Mother, somewhere in his head.

CHAPTER 26

At the white house with the green front door all was subdued. The only sound a frightened occasional mewing and clawing upstairs outside Greta's firmly shut door.

The house was very much in control. It had marshalled all of its might and force and cracks had sprung up in the boldest of places. The only place left damp, mould and mark free was just at the bottom of the stairs on the wall that housed Mother's painting. It knew to be careful in this space.

In front of Mother's portrait sat a wonderful display of violets and irises and oriental orchids, purples and pinks, with small touches of vibrant yellows and bright, bright white. It sparkled with vibrancy.

'It is the artist in you Charity, such a beautiful display.'

In the lounge the pictures of the family had been replaced by charming little sketches of mother and wildlife, the birds of course featuring rather prominently.

'Ahhh, won't little Harriet have a warm welcome home?'

'She is in the best place for now, we need to do more my dear.'

In Guy's living space, the girls had thrown back the

dark heavy curtains and allowed the light to once again fill the room. They had let in a little air to remove the cloying smell of disappointment and despair. A landscape from France had been replaced with a glorious violet, captured by Grace, which had been a gift for one of Mother's birthdays, she forgot which one. It didn't matter.

'Delightful dear.'

Some simple purple cushions and 'spit and polish' had transformed the room. The candles had been removed, the lampshades replaced with glass ones that refracted the light across the room, making it sparkle and some early spring daffodils had been placed on his desk. It seemed important that something living was put there.

The biggest change in the room was the removal of his special medicine.

'He is such a child.'

'And we must remember this is helpful.'

'Don't forget the brandy too dear, such an expense.'

'I'll take them to the attic, away from interference.'

The gramophone was in use now each day and the twins had taken to performing 'dance and movement' throughout the hallways and rooms. Each door was now wedged open, 'to allow us to breathe.'

The exercise would begin with star jumps, 11 to be exact, followed by 11 pirouettes and 11 touching of the toes. Then the music would begin and the free dance commenced, which was taken terribly seriously by the girls, who would simply move and sway to however the music took them. As long as it was performed with great gusto, the movements didn't matter.

'We are angels.'

Milly would venture down as soon as she heard the music and had learnt that the girls rarely leapt into the kitchen and so, she could drink from the sink and eat from whatever crumbs and leftovers she could find. A window was always ajar somewhere to 'dispel the poison,' and she could squeeze through and into the garden to catch what she could. The girls had moved the bird table from a dusty corner, given it a clean and it now stood in prime position in the centre of the garden, which Milly found was useful if she was hungry.

Harriet's bedroom had remained untouched, the door simply closed, but Guy's room had been opened up and the curtains removed. The light was allowed in and the windows opened, the air now billowed through the nets, disturbing his book which held his precious photograph. It lay on the floor along with an upturned old glass of wine which had slowly seeped through the pages, staining them and all it contained. A pinkish glow now stared out of the faces in the image, they looked slightly bloodied which was apt.

In her room, Greta groaned. How long had she been here? When did he leave, it seemed like an age. Certainly, three nights had past, she was counting the darkness each evening, and each morning she was amazed that she saw the daylight again. Her dreams were vivid, and she slept most of the day and awoke bathed anew in her own sweat.

It was usually the music that woke her, that infernal pounding beat, those high notes piercing in her head, the resulting thumps and bumps from below. Whatever were they doing?

She would try to call out, but was it her imagination or was the music played even louder when she did?

She was running out of water now, her jug with stale water was nearly empty and her mouth was so dry. Luckily, she had brought up a fresh one with her the day she felt unwell, so she had coped so far.

A little bit of strength came to her this morning and she lowered herself onto the floor, pulling herself along with her elbows, too tired and ill to be disgusted by the fowl soiled sheets and the filthy nightdress. She pulled herself along to the door and tried to reach up to the handle, but it was no good. It was too far out of reach and she had exhausted herself getting to it. Instead, she decided to sleep where she had landed curled up on the wooden floor. She was so feverish she didn't really notice the cold or miss her blankets although she was a bit concerned when her feet turned as blue as the twilight.

The blue hour was upon her.

She awoke very early the next morning. She knew it was dawn, as she watched the delicate winter colours dapple across the bedroom walls.

'Milly?'

She could hear her scratching just inches away from her.

'Milly, help me.'

It was ridiculous she knew, but just the sense of another living being nearby gave her some hope. As she reached out to try and get her fingers under the door, she knocked something with her elbow.

Biscuits! Three ginger biscuits lay on the floor, they must have been pushed through at some point whilst she slept. So, they didn't want her to die just yet.

'Thank you,' she said to the walls and bit into one of them and it was the sweetest most delicious taste she had ever experienced. She found it took her a long time to eat just one biscuit. There was so little moisture in her mouth, chewing and swallowing was difficult and after one she had so tired herself out that sleep took her again for a few hours before the music began once more

CHAPTER 27

Guy's meeting in Kendal had gone exceptionally well and Uncle William had agreed to leave his Scottish retreat and meet him at Carlisle on the borders.

Over a celebratory bottle of red, Uncle William reassessed his nephew. Without the girls, without the weight of that house, of that town; he seemed a jolly good chap. Less nervy, more robust somehow, even cracking the odd joke. It was rather a revelation.

'Bet you miss the boys eh?'

'The proud group of the fighting brotherhood, it can't be replaced can it? Women never quite understand do they old chap?'

'I didn't realise you fought Uncle. Important groundsman work I understood, too vital to let a chap like you go and get his head blown off.'

'Ahh well, some of us had to protect what we had you know, but damn shame I couldn't partake myself.'

Guy lit a cigar, took a large drink of wine and felt a million miles away from his war. Far removed from the cold, the fear and the smell of death all around him.

'Yes, I do miss a few of them, but I'm pleased to be back, one of the lucky ones and all that.'

'Yes, my boy of course,' and with that Uncle William

patted him on the back and ordered another bottle of wine. Maybe he could see his sister in this one after all. He was definitely from his side of the family he decided, absolutely one of them.

'Of course the girls still need me.'

'Yes, it was a valiant thing to do, to return after dear Hermione passed on.'

'Well Harriet especially needed me, it's very important to me that she stays safe, it can be such a difficult world out there, don't you agree Uncle?'

'Quite so Guy, the march of time as they say. And they are speaking about another war already, bloody nonsense!'

'I suppose they will ask you again if it happens eh, all your experience and knowledge, you'll be shipped off to Europe I'm sure.'

Guy didn't respond, he looked into his glass and was there with Cheri on the island. Her slim frame silhouetted in the window. She looked at him with that vacant look she had acquired in her last few months and smiled.

'It's time.'

'Yes, my dear.'

He watched his former self cross the room to her small blue cupboard with flowers painted on it, in the oriental fashion. She called it 'chinoiserie' and he loved the way her mouth made that sound. She reached into her pocket and brought out the key attached as always to the delphinium blue ribbon. Her favourite colour.

'You'll need this,' and she tossed the ribbon towards him. That beautiful blue which reminded him of the sea and the countryside around them.

And then as the mind is want to skip about, he was there at that rocky outcrop and Unity was splashing on the rocks, waving to him, laughing. He felt the sun on his neck; with another sip of the wine he was on the beach having a picnic. There was bread, cheese, olives, island salt and the wine, always the wine. He licked his lips.

Uncle William and Guy sat for a while in compatible silence. Uncle William quite reassured that the business would be in safe hands with Guy and even more reassured that he would hold onto Harriet until she was old enough to leave home, no doubt about it.

'How is the girl? Such a dreadful accident.'

'She is getting along fine Uncle; the rest home is in a beautiful spot.'

'Yes, I really must make the time to see her, but you know how it is so dreadfully busy.'

Of course, he had no intention of visiting his niece and had tied himself up in pointless commitments to make sure he couldn't. Guy was well aware of his uncles' ways. He was quite like the twins in that respect, just couldn't cope with illness or suffering, didn't quite understand it, and certainly didn't want it to encroach on his life.

'Well Uncle, she must rest at the moment so maybe now is not quite the right time to see her.'

'Whatever you think best my boy, she is lucky to have you as a brother, jolly good show. Just give me the nod though won't you.'

'Of course.'

Both were satisfied with their chat and the outcome. Guy would be the only one to see Harriet and Uncle did not have to trouble himself any further.

It was with a mixture of trepidation and urgency that Guy bade William goodbye and made his return journey. She had been without him for over a week now. Maybe Harriet had already forgotten Unity and the lake. He knew his sister could be a little flighty at times. He hoped he hadn't left it too long.

On arrival at the lake house, he was asked to wait once more and once more he took himself down to the water's edge to look out at the place that his daughter had grown to love. He wasn't surprised at her choice of location, she had always loved the water, delighted in it.

'It is too deep mon cher.'

He wiped Cheri's voice from his mind and in a flash and a shake of the head, his wife had gone.

'Daddy's here darling, come and say hello.'

The water was glassy today not even the faintest ripple on the surface, hardly any wind, very different conditions.

'I'll be back dear, don't disappear now.'

As he walked back to the house, he thought that maybe she had decided not to make friends with his sister after all, maybe the only reason she spoke to her was to give him credibility. Yes, that was it, she was just looking after her old Pa.

Something made him look up at the window and there was Harriet pointing at him. He lifted a hand to wave.

'Harriet darling.'

She continued pointing to the little girl on the rock out in the water, who was saying the same thing to her as she had every day since she first saw her.

'Sshhhh,' the noise came in waves to her as she slept.

But Guy didn't turn around, he rushed inside and knocked on the doctor's room, desperate now to talk to his sister.

Enclosed in the forest green room and sitting on his swivel chair, the man who was apparently so adept at the nuances of human behaviour, spoke to the other man who wished he wasn't quite so painfully aware.

'She is still a little non-responsive Mr Leighton, I'm afraid to say. On the plus side there are no lingering physical after effects from her dip in the cold lake. As a precaution however we haven't allowed her outside since the incident or indeed left her alone at all other than for sleeping of course. This is the point at which we apply the straps, to keep her in her bed, as sleep really is the most important thing, isn't it?'

Maybe then Unity was just waiting, if she hadn't even had the chance to be near the lake again? And he doubted very much that his darling daughter would visit this unknown lakeside house.

'So, she hasn't been outside all week doctor?'

'No and I think it best that we stick to the same routine a little while longer, until she becomes more of her old self again.'

'And the opiates?'

'On a very mild dose now, which we hope to begin to cut very soon, it just helps to relax her at the moment. We mustn't forget what an awful trauma she suffered.'

'Are the strappings necessary?'

'It's common practice after an 'episode' that protects all of us you understand.'

'Can I see her today doctor?'

'Yes Mr Leighton we are interested to see if meeting a loved one, will affect her mood, we hope it may raise the spirits.'

Guy rather hoped so too.

Both men stood and made their way up the mahogany staircase. Harriet was housed near the top of the building and Guy found himself wheezing on reaching the top.'

'The gas you know,' spoke the war hero.

'Of course.'

Harriet was sitting on a simple wooden chair. The room was very hot, and a fire burned in the grate and he could see that the windows were nailed down. Still she looked out over the water and seemed to shiver a little despite being wrapped in a blanket in the heat.

'Harriet dear you have a visitor.'

'I know.'

'Harry darling, it's me, how are you? You gave me quite a fright.'

'I bet.'

Harriet turned to look at him now and was surprised

at what she felt. She had spent the feverish nights troubled and frightened of this man and yet looking at him now, she felt the overriding love she always had.

'Could we have a moment alone doctor?'

He nodded and motioned to the nurse, 'we will just be outside, ten minutes.'

He took her in his arms and held her. He felt her body tense, then relax and then relax even more until she was slipping from his hold.

'Harry?'

He put her back in her chair and he joined her looking out onto the water.

'What did you do?'

'Ahh Harry, I've only ever wanted you all to be safe.'

He kissed her forehead and she looked at him and felt a numbness and inevitability.

'What did you do?' Quietly spoken now.

'She's still with us, you know that don't you Harriet?'

She nodded, and he smiled and gathered up his belongings.

'It's because I love you.'

Outside with the doctor he asked if they could talk downstairs.

'I'm still a little concerned doctor.'

'Of course you are, it must still be a shock.'

'You mentioned electroconvulsive treatment?'

'Yes, but I'm not sure we are at that stage yet and there is a danger of course that we remove a part of her memory and we can't of course, pick and choose which parts.'

'I see, thank you doctor, well I really should leave now.'

And with that Guy made his way out of the door, satisfied that he was not alone, was not imagining any of it, was as healthy and sane as the next man and if Harriet did forget, well that wasn't such a terrible thing. He had

189

received confirmation this morning and that was something. Something rather terrific.

He did a little skip and high kick on the last step.

He had a delay at Lancaster. Damn! He would have to stay overnight, and he so wanted to return home and prepare the house for Harriet. After his experiences with the maid, he also wondered about Greta, maybe it wouldn't be so difficult to love again? Greta was small and fair like Cheri, this both troubled and delighted him.

There was something else too, Greta was one of those pure souls and he was a little afraid of her because of this. He felt as complicated as the darkest night.

It may all be difficult again, and he wasn't sure he was ready for another person wanting every last bit of him. Later, he would see. For now, he needed sleep. He cabled the twins and turned in for the night.

CHAPTER 28

'Charity, he is on his way.'

'We must be firm dear, we can't lose the light now.'

'Yes, Mother would think it was for the best.'

'Of course, she would. Will you sort out Greta? I don't think I could again after yesterday. It feels like such a terrible risk even going near her door.'

'I suppose that is only fair. Obscene isn't it, still needs must.'

'Remember to hold your breath and wear your scarf around your face dear. I'll help you scrub yourself afterwards.'

Grace went into the pantry and found the biscuits and as she was there wondered if perhaps Greta may be ready for milk. It was only then that it struck her that perhaps she hadn't had anything to drink for all the time she was up there.

'Charity, Charity! Drink, we haven't given her anything to drink.'

'Calm down Grace, the Leighton family do not panic.'

'Maybe the stench confused us?'

'That dear is the filth of illness, we have done the right thing. We need to contain these things. Vigilance is key.

It cannot spread, there is too much at stake.'

'Let's go up there together this time. Prepare yourself.'

And with that the twins took a jug of water and glass of milk along with the biscuits and stood on Greta's landing listening. The cat was still sitting outside, but it ran and hid as soon as she heard them.

'It's quiet Charity, I can't hear a thing.'

'Well go and listen at the door.'

'Is that not too close?'

'Just try not and touch anything.'

Grace tiptoed, which was a sensation that felt odd in itself. No one normally warranted such strange behaviour, forthright was her default setting. How she was changing these past few months!

The smell was overwhelming and made Grace convulse and heave a little, she brought her scarf up to her face and hoped the germs could not travel under the door. She gave herself a mental note to leave her shoes outside for three days in the air.

She shook her head and Charity joined her, also with scarf applied to nose and mouth. She turned the lock and felt a weight as she pushed the door.

'Is she breathing?'

The door opened only a little way with Greta's body slumped against it, but it was enough.

'Don't touch her dear.'

'She is breathing. See how her body rises and falls.'

'Well reach through and place the jug and milk down, I've brought extra biscuits today.'

'Do hurry dear and then shut the door, it's really intolerable.'

And with that the girls took themselves outside, stripped off their clothes and stood outside in the icy cold rain.

It was the smoke that woke Greta up, burning outside her window, weaving its way through the cracks to her nose and mouth. The adrenaline surge that this caused, was enough to heave herself off the floor and to the window.

Outside she saw the girls, without a stitch on, burning their clothes in the decorative chimney pot. Extraordinary, what on earth were they doing? It was so very cold outside; she tried to open the window some more, but she wasn't strong enough.

'Milk! is that milk?'

She saw the glass on the floor and the jug and yet more biscuits, they had been in the room.

Greta dived on the drink, but found that after a few big gulps she felt quite sick and so after a while, slowly dipped the biscuits into the milk which seemed to help her digest it. After, she felt a little less light headed, but the tiredness returned and she dragged herself into the vile stained bed. She was past caring, and sleep hit her like a freight train.

'How disappointing Grace, we should have thought more clearly. I'm furious with myself. It's such a shame to see the cream cowl dress disappear into flames. It was by Lanvin you know.'

'We are not risking infection Charity, not after everything we've all been through. It's much better this way and we are beautiful enough for it not to matter, we don't need designer wear now do we?'

It was said without a jot of irony. The girls only dealt in the facts as they saw them, and in a way it was true, they were undeniably beautiful.

They made their sodden way inside and ran a 'cleansing boiling hot Dettol bath,' and stayed in it, until it stung and burnt, and all of Greta's unpleasantness had gone. No living thing, especially not an infection could survive the Leighton thorough clean.

'Cleanliness is next to Godliness.'

'Heat and air nature's helpers.'

'He will be here tomorrow lunchtime, dear.'

'Do we need to do anything else?'

'No, let's enjoy ourselves this evening and make Mother proud.'

They managed to make their own supper, in itself a magnificent result. They ate it off the special Christmas plates which featured such a cheerful scene. There was no need for the duck egg plates any more.

They took a sherry each into Guy's old sitting room, which had now very much returned to the house. The girls opened the curtains to let in the moonlight, and felt it absorbing through their pores. They sang mother's favourite songs to bring her back where she belonged.

'There is poetry and song to all of this.'

'It is, it is.'

CHAPTER 29

A man of renewed vitality and purpose stepped from the platform at Royal Leamington Spa and made the walk to his home. He took the longer route through the pump room gardens, over the river and past the bandstand. It was a bright day and so he decided that rather than walk straight up Newbold Street, he would walk through the Jephson's gardens and admire the fountains.

The resident heron swooped past him as he entered the park through the wrought iron gates as if to guide him home. Past the flower beds, too early for any spring colour, and onward past the now quiet aviary. He felt no need to linger at that spot anymore.

'Better this way.'

Past the clock tower and through the gates at the other side and there he was, a man looking at his house at the end of the row of white buildings, none of which had a front door painted as vibrantly green as his own.

He pushed the door but found it was shut, 'tsk.' The girls knew he was coming, was he not the returning hero? The business man returning home having secured their future.

He tried his key, 'well how very odd indeed.' Finding that the key didn't work, he resorted to his final option and rang the bell. What a bright and cheerful sound!

Then there was nothing. No footsteps, no voices, no

sound in fact at all. An absence.

Guy waited a while on the step, not quite sure what to do. Even if Greta was out and about, it was most unusual for his sisters to leave the building; they were so like their mother in that respect.

He leaned over the railings and looked into his sitting room, the first thing that shocked him was that the curtains were open and even the window ajar. He tried to peer further inside but couldn't quite reach. He had seen enough, there was such an overriding sense of differentness.

'Grace!'

'Charity!'

There was no response, so he waited five minutes longer, then turning on his heel he made his way to the public house on the corner. He would simply have to wait, how very thoughtless of them. Still, he wasn't particularly surprised. They rarely considered anyone else and didn't really work to a structured timescale.

'Lost, they are lost,' he said to his pint of ale.

Upstairs the girls lay on the floor and did something quite extraordinary for them. They laughed, loud and uncontrollably, rolling around in absolute delight, quite unable to contain themselves.

Wattle, wattle and wattle.

The house had been claimed.

Mother glowed from her portrait in the hall.

The noise woke Greta too, her mind had become a little clearer since her last sleep. Less foggy and firmer footed, she managed to swing her feet onto the floor and stand. Baby steps yet it made her feel hopeful. Greta realised she would need to try and pick her moment to get out of the room and seek help.

The twins would not rescue her. Biscuits and milk were of little help to her, if she was to regain her full strength. They could just about keep her alive, but she was weak as a kitten and would remain so without outside help. How she longed for Harriet and Guy to return, but she though that would be some time yet, and time was not particularly on her side.

Hope could be a dangerous thing.

. . .

From his position in the Newbold Arms he could see his street, see who ventured up and down. He was sure at any moment Greta would appear around the corner carrying groceries and he would be able to swoop in, carry her bag and carry on where he left off. The thought rather excited him.

He felt like he was due a reward.

After some basic food, bread cheese and pickle and another drink, he felt he would try his luck again. No one had ventured forth yet, and it was becoming ridiculous.

'Greta, it's me Guy.'

His knocking grew more and more insistent. He had dispensed with the cheerful sounding bell. It didn't have the required gravitas.

'Girls, it's your brother, do come along.'

He imagined them upstairs in the attic painting furiously away, more twisted sinewy paintings no doubt, oblivious to anything else.

The house had become a fortress and it braced itself for what was to come.

There was beauty and there was light within. It was a prize for the taking.

CHAPTER 30

The pub was shut for a few hours when he returned.
'Damn and blast.'

He had no option but to take a turn around the town,
perhaps he would venture to the chemist – just in case.
He was sure he had a prescription on him somewhere. It
was lucky he had his travelling bag with him, Guy never
knew what to expect when away from home, so caution
necessitated quite a long list of items.

Walking to Dunns on Regent Street, he handed in his
prescription. They knew him here, he still had some
standing in the town, despite him marrying a French
woman and having a German work for him rather than
one of their own. His family name had carried all of them
and his beautiful celebrated sisters was ensuring the great
Leightons were still respected. He begrudgingly had to
give them some credit for this, even if they were not in
charge of their own beauty, they nourished it and that
could be helpful.

'Dazzle, steal hearts and win my treasures,' said
Mother in his head.

'My usual please Sarah.'

'Ahh Mr Leighton, how are you and the family? We
were so sorry to hear of young Harriet's trouble.'

Of course, they all knew and he expected the gossip would be wild fire across the county.

'Have they caught whoever did it Sir?'

'Of course, it's none of my business, only we were all so concerned.'

'Not yet, no, but we do so appreciate your concern, I'll make sure to tell Harriet when I see her next'

'And the girls, it must be such a strength that you all have each other?'

'Have you seen them at all lately?'

'No sir, but then that's not unusual is it Mr Leighton, they must have so many other important things to do.'

'Yes, of course.'

'Why not take them some chocolate, on us, help to cheer you all up.' Sarah reached for two bars of Fry's chocolate cream and popped them in the bag.

'That's most generous thank you, we will all appreciate it very much.'

'I'll take some of the tincture too if I may, Grace does have a terrible cold, I think it may be the stress of everything, you know how it can be.'

'Maybe some cough drops too? The strong ones are best I think.'

When he had his parcel, he thought he would need to warm up, so he took himself up the graceful Parade with all the Regency buildings, so like his own house. His own house, damn it! He took refuge in the Cadena café.

'Mr Leighton, nice to see you here.'

A man Guy hadn't seen before, came out to meet him, clearing the best table in the window for him, which he took thankfully, inwardly smiling. Amazing how a relatively small event could move people.

'Soft dear, quite soft in the head.' said Mother.

After the war everything seemed so insignificant to him. I mean who really cared about other people? Quite extraordinary, but then he supposed they were celebrities of a fashion.

'My name's Ted, sir. Greta and Harriet used to sometimes call in for pikelets and tea.'

'Pleased to meet you Ted. In that case I'll have the same.'

Was it his imagination or did the man even blush? Honestly! Still he would most probably get his pikelets on the house and as things were that was a jolly good thing.

As he gazed out of the window, his mind took the opportunity to wander a little and instead of the cold icy, snow flurry sort of a Warwickshire day, he was on the island in the, 'Bar tabac de blu.'

Cheri and him, were sitting in a sun hazed corner gazing outwards, and he smiled at the memory. There were the dark wooden chairs, the glass ash tray and the smell of the absinthe Cheri had so grown to love. He drank his pastis as usual, he loved the way it turned cloudy after adding water. It reminded him of old school science experiments and the little bit of the young boy that remained delighted each time. He wasn't even sure he particularly liked the rough aniseed taste, but it wasn't about that. None of it was.

Orange blossom caught him off-guard on the breeze.

'Un instant ma chère.'

Cheri excused herself and he followed her slim frame with his tired eyes. The bones in her wrist were particularly prominent as he watched her greet the man that had entered the café. Her hands gripped his shoulder as she kissed him on the cheek, like talons gripping prey.

'Guy,' she pronounced it 'Gee' which usually annoyed him, but today after his pastis, he didn't mind quite so much.

'Jean, un autre verre s'il vous plait.'

And so, another round of absinthe arrived. He sipped tentatively at his, it always gave him such a terrible headache and he still had to be a responsible carer at some point, even if she couldn't care less. When she ordered she would always order him her drink. He used to think this was charming and rather bold. He used to rather enjoy being 'Gee.'

In chilly Leamington Spa, he realised she and his mother were disturbingly alike. Mother would have been furious at the suggestion.

Cheri was now on her third drink and her eyes were very glazed and she was becoming more flirtatious. There would be no especial need for her little routine tonight and that was a small blessing.

He always wondered why this business arrangement had to take place so publicly and why did it have to be so protracted. There was always drinks, then the walk on the beach.

Maybe that was why he now preferred a discreet delivery in an unmarked package. Far more dignified.

'Un cadeau pour moi?' She giggled.

'Mais oui, mon fleur.' He stroked her face, which Guy didn't like, but Cheri did. It made her simper, her mouth red and pouting, her cheekbones even more noticeable, only her eyes were dead.

No small achievement.

They thanked Madame Rousseau, who smiled at them with knowing sad eyes and they took their turn on the beach. Guy, not such an absinthe regular, was thankfully numbed to the worst of the spectacle.

Once they were alone, Jean handed her the box which he had even bothered to tie with a huge blue bow.

'Ahh delphinium, Guy how he remembers, non?'

She embraces this man in his cartoon Breton top and he feels like he shouldn't be there to witness this, but he does, of course. He stands there and waits for her, feeling redundant and emasculated.

'Mummy's little pansy.'

He watches this man's arms encircle her, his hands resting on her hips nonchalantly as if it were the most normal thing in the world. She presses her body into his, the hands that were on the hip grasp a little tighter, the thumbs pressing into her crotch. She laughs her raspy waspish little giggle and at that moment Guy hates her with such a dangerous passion, but it is transitory. She stares at Guy whilst pressed into this other man. The stare is so intense that Guy can feel Jean's erection pulsing through the soft folds in his own thigh.

He kisses her neck, seemingly unaware that her husband stands there watching. But, this is not polite society.

She arches backwards, and he moves to her breasts, which she offers up eagerly. All the time she and Guy watch each other. He has the good grace not to enter her there and then, it is enough.

As he walks past Guy on his way back to the road, he nods a cheery 'au revoir.' Guy returns the words and feels no malice. It is what it is.

It is, it is, it is.

Once Jean has left, he goes to her and now she wants to swim.

'To see my little girl, where she waits under the waves.'

'She is a little mermaid now.'

'Come to mama mon petite.'

She is waist height before he sighs and wades out to get her. He feels no pleasure as he holds her taught bony frame, but she wants to kiss him, and he wonders when this absence of feeling arrived.

Cheri is hanging around his neck now, but he holds her firm and manages to navigate her back onto the land. He is exhausted, the water making even her a heavy weight. Now she is crying and calling the child's name over and over again.

It is a long evening, n'est-ce pas?

Once on the beach, they disentangle and walk back to their rooms in silence leaving a briny sea water trail behind them. Guy knows that no amount of mind-numbing suppression is going to make this evening be alright. It is becoming something of a habit now. The first drink perks them up a little and then they have too many, sometimes they fight, mostly he can't be bothered.

He climbs into bed and tries to look like he is asleep, but she is wise to him and he feels cold metal brush past his nose and then clank down onto the wooden floorboards. He ignores it. But that won't do, he can hear her, smell her, salty and seaweedy from the beach below him. She grapples under the bed, until she has it in her hand. She moves and kneels besides his side of the bed. He can smell her breath now, putrid and decaying from lack of food and too much everything else. Still he keeps his eyes shut.

'Guy'

'Mon amour'

'Geeeeeeeee'

'Guy!'

Like an animal he can feel her eyes needy and wanting on his, beady in the night time, wanting, scratching and devouring him.

Still he won't open his eyes.

He feels the ribbon tickle his nose and she is giggling now, that giggle that was so charming, so vibrant and full of promise, now just sounds scratchy, hollow and rough.

'Dah-ling.'

The double emphasis, he used to love it, now it makes him so uncomfortable, sing song and slightly ever so sinister.

''My English boy.'

Then the metal is in his eyes trying to pierce open his eyelids. The animal won't rest, just like a cat pawing and tormenting her prey.

So, he grabs her thin skeletal hand and forces it back and she is on her back on the floor laughing.

He grabs the key, walks over to her special cupboard and pours her more than he should of medicine.

'Thank you.'

'Thank you Mr Leighton, sir and give my best to your sisters.'

Back in the Cadena café, a steaming pot of tea arrives, and he helps himself to too much sugar as if the sweetness can dissolve the memories. He tucks into his pikelets and finds he is ravenous, even wiping the dripping butter with his fingers and licking them. He had his back to the room, no-one could really see, he tells himself.

Guy takes his time sitting in the room that his sister used to so enjoy the company of the man that served him. He notices people smiling at him and raising their hat or their hand in greeting, solemn looks all round. He had no idea how popular the family were. He supresses a giggle.

Fortified, he returns to the cold streets, just as another snow flurry sparks up and he makes his way along the Parade and back to the Newbold Arms.

They are just opening as he arrives. He walks past his house first of course and see's no-one, not a sausage. It is getting dark, but he can't see any lights on yet. Is it possible that they are away?

Resigned, he asks for a room for the night.

'I have some important work to do and really can't be disturbed at home.'

The barman smiles to himself, he gets lots of gentlemen with the same predicament and leads him up the dark cold stairs to a small box room at the back, cheerless and with no view of the house.

Once ensconced in his room, he removes his coat and on the small dressing table he lines up his evening necessities. Out comes the medicine, followed by the tincture, then the cough drops and finally some alcohol all lined up with exactly the same distance between them.

He will begin at 10pm as is his usual practice.

'Good night mon cher.'

And his last thoughts of the day aren't with his sisters and the house and Leamington Spa but to Cheri and her delphinium blue ribbon. Still clutched tight in her fist as she lies unmoving on the floor; the bright summer sun seeping in through the slatted blinds, drawing stripes over her thin, bruised legs.

CHAPTER 31

All is now quiet over the road at the white house with the green front door. Greta wakes and finds some more biscuits have been shoved under the door and more milk. It will do. Once she has eaten them slowly and carefully, she picks up her nail scissors and tries the door. She steels herself to have to kick at the lock and push with all her might, but it opens at the gentlest touch.

'Is it a trick?'

Standing in the corridor now, she is all alone, no sound. The twins don't appear and force her back to bed. It's dark as she walks along the hall and she wonders if it is morning at all, how long has she slept? She has forgotten to dress and is still in her soiled nightdress and bare feet. Her hair unwashed for days now, lies lank and greasy against her head. She doesn't care, she didn't expect to get this far at all and she isn't about to stop – not now she has come this far.

Silence.

Greta stands still, her breathing laboured. She tries her best to steady herself, takes a deep breath, but this makes a pain sear through her chest and she doubles over.

Still all is quiet and this makes the sound of the blood rushing in her head even louder. There is life!

One foot now appears in front of the other and small

shaky steps are made.

'Maybe I can do this!'

She leaves her body for a moment and appears to watch herself as she crawls slowly along the corridor.

'Slowly, slowly, catchy monkey,' says a distant far away Guy.

Greta's body is wrecked and tired and she almost doesn't recognise the person creeping along a hallway that she used to march along. At least then she was confident in her body's ability to do the basic act of walking. Now, all is confusion and bones.

She stops again and listens. Nothing, so on she continues with her slow and painful progress.

She stumbles a little as she turns the bend in the hall. Greta is caught off guard by the many faces of the children's mother. So many different studies, so many. The woman in the drawings looks out at Greta quizzically, as if she shouldn't be there.

'I'm going now,' whispers Greta.

'About time dear,' says Mother.

Her head spins as she stands at the foot of the stairs looking down. It's dark down there too, but she can see a small flicker of light coming from Guy's study.

'Oh! He's home, he's here!'

'That's why the door is unlocked, he must have just arrived, Guy...'

Still cautious, Greta took an apprehensive move down onto the first step. She felt even dizzier, but she had done it.

'Well done Greta, only a few more steps, come on.' she chivvies herself in her best strict voice.

She grabs at the bannister as she makes her slow tenuous progress down the stairs, Mother looks on from the big painting in the hallway, watchful now.

'Be patient, I'll be out soon.'

'Nearly there.'

On the bottom step she trips and lies at the foot of the stairs. No one comes, but she must have made a sound as she fell in an awkward, ugly and twisted heap. Surely that must have made an almighty racket, why hasn't anyone appeared? Maybe no one is here at all, and this thought galvanises Greta forward.

She twists her painful bruised neck and looks up, there are lots of cracks in the celling, and one is right above her head, streaked with a poisonous mould. She lies very still and traces its progress with her eyes.

'It's all fallen apart,' she whispers into the ether and she feels the house respond with a hairline splinter forming from the crack, followed by another one and again one more.

The guardians must be away or busy elsewhere for the house to dare a chance.

'I'll soon be leaving,' she whispers again and a tear forms in her eye, but it hasn't the strength to leave her eye socket and it momentarily blinds her, filling it up. From somewhere deep inside she musters energy to blink it away and the portrait smiles at her.

'I tried my best.'

'Goodbye.'

She hasn't the strength to stand anymore. Instead she manages to slowly roll her body onto her side, rest a while, then onto her front, and up onto her elbows. In that position she manages to drag herself towards Guy's room, pulling her poor exhausted body over the parquet floor.

'One way to dust it,' she thinks. Greta remembers how long it used to take her to buff this hallway and she remembers herself then, only a few weeks ago. Beautiful and in love, dressed impeccably; she heard her own laugh in her head, it sounded incredibly foreign now and unrecognisable.

The world can change in a heartbeat. The changes

sneak up bit by bit and then it's adapt or die. It seems sudden, but the story is set long before.

Does it help to know this? Probably, probably not. It doesn't make for an easy character.

Greta sees wet streaks on the floor behind her and she realises it is her lumpen mass and she is damp and cloying. The exertion had brought her out into a rancid sweat and she smelt like everything was wrong and that seemed about right.

'Come on.'

She felt Mother's eyes follow her and will her on, out of the house.

'There is nothing I want more.'

Resting, prostrate on the floor for a moment, she could hear whispering, but she wasn't sure if this was in her head or real voices. Nothing made any sense any more.

Pulling together all of her strength, she raised herself up on her elbows once more, which were now cracked and bleeding and continued on towards the room.

It was open when she finally reached it. The flickering light was candlelight and from her position on the floor, she could see them. Both girls were sitting in a circle with two empty chairs, their hands holding the air and outstretched, as if holding hands with another who was unseen.

'He's not here dear.'

'And we don't expect him back.'

They knew she was there! And yet she didn't move, fear and a new searing pain in her legs left her quite incapable.

'You've been such a long time Greta and we just couldn't wait.'

They didn't look at her and spoke with their eyes shut. Greta rolled over and curled herself up in a ball, still in the doorway. With no strength to speak she just lay there, watching.

'She's here now Grace.'

'So, we can carry on.'

'You must be quiet Greta, not a squeak.'

She wouldn't make a sound, even if she could. All that effort and what had she had achieved? A different room, but it was unlikely that she would leave the house after all now. She was sure that they wouldn't let her go. She didn't understand that she wasn't the prisoner, rather it was she who had held them captive. Greta realised that Guy hadn't come to rescue her, and more moisture filled her eyes and this time fell down her cheeks and yet she made no sound.

Light seemed to stream in suddenly from underneath the door. It started at the bottom and slowly rose to fill the hallway. It was a full moon, 'of course,' thought Greta, 'of course.'

It illuminated everything. The pictures that spoke from the walls, the cracks in the ceiling, her own filthy smears on the floor. Greta could see the blood in it, visceral and inevitable.

'No going back,' she mouthed.

And then as quickly as it came, it was gone, as a cloud passed over the face of the moon, that lit the big white house with the green front door.

'Begin Charity.'

'Come and talk to us Mummy.'

'Mummy, it's time you came back fully.'

'We know he was very naughty.'

'Let us know dear.'

A sound like breaking glass and Greta saw one of the girl's drawings of their mother lie on the floor, it must have fallen.

'Thank you.'

'Gracious as always.'

Greta watched silently, painfully and was fully

absorbed. 'They have lost their minds; the dead do not speak.'

She looked at them, heads were hung down, and Grace's was lolling to one side, both of them with a smile etched on their beautiful faces.

'What should we do?'

Again, the sound of more smashing glass as another picture fell from the walls.

'This is insane,' thought Greta, I must get out whilst they are occupied. 'I need to try one more time.'

The candles flickered, the poor damaged wrists clicked, and the legs jiggered in the big white house with the green front door.

On shaky legs she managed to heave herself up against a chair.

'Shhhhhh Greta.'

It stilled her for a moment, they knew she was still there, she thought they were too caught up in their magic to notice, but it wasn't the case.

'What did he do?'

She waited and as the next picture fell, threw herself against the door frame. She wanted to scream out and yell as she whacked her wrecked body onto the wood, but she mustn't.

'Do tell us Mummy.'

'What dear, Grace there is someone else with us?'

A glass of water at Charity's side shattered to the floor and in time Greta dragged herself around the door and back into the hall. She could drag herself against the wall now, all the way to the front door. 'You can do this,' she told herself, 'You have to.'

'Ahh hello child, we don't see you very often.'

But Greta couldn't see them anymore, had no idea who or what they were now talking about or too, did not care. She was focussed on her task, which was to get out of that door, nothing else at that moment mattered. She still didn't understand that they didn't mind one jot.

Light streamed through the house again as another cloud passed over exposing the streaks of blood and sweat now in stripes across the wall. It another world it was rather pretty.

'What did he do?'

Another glass smashed and she heard water drip. She was on the door handle now, she had to summon all her strength to drag the bolts across. Greta managed it, but the door was still locked and she had no idea where the key was. She held her breath and then…

'Think Greta, think.'

'What did he do?'

Greta heard the twins asking the same question over and over again, with more insistence each time. She heard knocking on the wood and could only imagine they were now rocking their chairs as she heard a scraping scratching sound but she was pleased with the noise, as it meant she had a distraction.

The umbrella stand!

And with that she reached out and made it to the base of the large Chinese vase that they used for umbrellas and sticks. Where was it?

The knocking sounds became louder and so she took her cue and with great necessity she pushed against the vase watching it tumble in slow motion, before it fell crashing to the ground.

Silence, no knocking, no words. Greta took her chance and adrenaline surged into her body allowing her to scrabble around in the now broken china until the key unearthed itself. She cut herself, but by now she didn't mind about more blood, what did a bit more matter?

'Haaarrrieettttttttttttttttt.' The voices were strange, not like the twins at all. The noise was guttural and other worldly. The name was screamed out loud, it splintered through Greta's mind and key now in hands she made for the lock and did what she so needed to do.

Open.

And the cold air hit her sharply and she couldn't breathe. Snow was lying on the steps and she stood there in her soiled nightdress and bare feet looking out into the night.

She stepped out of the only home she had known for such a very long time and stood on the step. Greta was pleased that the snow hid her red and raw feet. A gust of freezing night air whipped through her thin cotton dress, past her tired old bones and into the house and with that there was a loud bang and the door slammed shut.

Terrified that the twins would come outside and find her, she threw herself down the steps and dragged herself through the snow to the park gates and the main road gasping and spluttering, it wasn't long before she lost consciousness. Harrington House with its turrets and dark splendour loomed in the inky black.

She didn't understand that her leaving was the best gift that the girls could receive.

'Slam dunk darlings.'

CHAPTER 32

Some hours later and it was Greta's turn to be a patient in the Warnford hospital. A kindly nurse sat and held her hand.

'What's your name dear?'

'Can you try very hard to remember?'

Greta looked at the red cheeked round woman talking to her. She smelt disinfectant and saw she was wearing a gown. It was comforting, so she squeezed her hand and fell back to sleep.

It was quiet back at the house too, the twins had fallen asleep in their chairs after the night's activities. Sunlight streaming into the house promised new beginnings and it was Grace who first opened up her eyes.

'We are free.'

'We just need our girl back.'

'Nearly there.'

She looked around and smiled at the broken glass, the pictures lying on the floor, the blood on the wall. Tsk, that was Greta of course, so selfish at times that girl. All in all, it had been a most successful experience.

It was with a renewed sense of purpose that the girls took to cleaning the room, broken glass was swept away, walls were splashed and rubbed with disinfectant and the curtains opened to allow the light to flood through the house and with each encroaching ray of sunlight the dirt was bleached clean away.

'We need to venture into Greta's room dear, I can't bear to think of it, but we must rid the last of the infection.'

'Yes, we must be terribly brave mustn't we, after all we have done much worse to get everything in order haven't we now.'

'The mess in the hallway too Charity, we must get every last piece of the germs out of the house before we get her.'

Another fire was lit in the garden and everything including the cat's blanket was burnt until there was no trace.

Once the girls had tended to the dreaded THINGS, they ran a Dettol bath and each one scrubbed the other until their alabaster skin turned red and sore.

'That's better.'

And they lay in their bedroom with the windows wide open to get what force was left of the waning moon.

Guy, having spent the day in utter frustration at not getting into the house had decided to call Uncle William and had sent a telegram. Other than trying the house a few times, he had taken to his bed and taken as much medicine as he dared and found it helped with the dreaded thoughts that came so freely now and urgently. No longer were they simply contained to night time or the odd sighting, it was becoming increasingly difficult to tell where he was and who he was with. The rational mind that was left told him to try and sleep, it was the stress and he would be better alone for a day or two.

Greta also slept. She slept soundly for 16 hours and only awoke as they roused her to make her eat. She found she was ravenous and devoured the egg and bread that she was given. This time her food stayed down and with that she fell into sleep again, quite unable to speak or in any way engage with the staff looking after her.

'The fever has a while yet to run its course.'

At dawn the front door of the house with the green front door was flung open and a resplendent Grace, stepped over the threshold in white furs. The cold air rather pleased her and she smiled up at the snow filled clouds that would cover her stride.

She liked to feel a little invisible, it somehow made her feel invincible.

As Mother always said, 'stealth, will provide my girls, don't you forget it.'

She had walked to the railway station, it was so simple now, there was no need pretending that she was a silly girl that needed assistance. No-one watching her or questioning her.

Her brother could be a terrible bore.

There was no one in the ticket office when she arrived, but someone at least was available to pour her a cup of tea whilst she waited for her train. Grace often found that the menfolk of Leamington Spa were incredibly kind and accommodating.

'Extraordinary that civilisation doesn't seem to trouble itself before 7am.'

The purr of the steam train, the jump of the guard, the slamming of a door, the blow of a whistle, the 'let me help you madam,' and she was seated at the window, the only person in her carriage.

It was lunchtime when she arrived and stepped from the train in the unknown village.

'The Lake House please.'

He admired her beauty and was incredibly helpful and courteous, in the way that men anywhere often are in the face of such things. Couldn't imagine what such a special lady was doing up at that place with its stories and going-ons.

To say he was bowled over by the woman standing before him was understated to say the least. He shuffled his feet and found it difficult to meet her eye.

On arrival, Grace took in her surroundings. It seemed more than adequate but it wasn't home. And home, was now where her sister needed to be.

'I'm here to bring my sister home,' said a triumphant Grace.

'I'm afraid I have not met your acquaintance before,' said the quiet mumbling man.

'The name is Leighton and my sister is Harriet, would you be so kind as to fetch her for me.'

She smiled the smile she felt was appropriate for the situation and realised that she may have to lightly touch this man's arm if he seemed reluctant to do as she asked.

An inward little shudder took her momentarily.

'We were not expecting you? Your brother seemed concerned that she should rest some more.'

'Ahh Guy is such a worry wort,' and then lightly touching his arm and leaning in towards the individual;

'He has some troubles of his own you know, and you have my personal reassurance she will be taken care of.'

'Let me fetch her Miss Leighton, it is Miss, isn't it?' he mumbled, 'not Mrs? Well, I shan't be a moment.'

'Grace, please,' she said, and 'very much alone in the world,' and again her most devastating smile that would help no end.

'Sparkle and dazzle and disarm.'

A somewhat subdued Harriet was brought into the room alongside a man, with 'Dr' on his name badge. Harriet's surprise to see her sister was obvious.

'You…came.'

'Of course dear, it's time to take you home.'

Grace felt the doctor's eyes on her and as such drew her sister into her arms. She could wash Harriet's dribble and tears off her in the wash room, but needs must. Typical of Harriet to target her no longer pristine white fur wrap. She must end the hug, for fear of mottling.

'Thank you.' Harriet repeated over and over again.

Grace pulled her from her, held her at arm's length and gave her a good look up and down.

'Is she quite all right Doctor?'

Smiling, he reassured Grace that the love of her family was all she needed. He was pleased the sister had come, the brother had seemed to have interesting characteristics of his own, but this vision before him, was one of those extraordinary people who held not just beauty, but a certain class and sensibility. He found he was a terribly good judge of people, well in his game he simply had to be.

'We would of course like to review Harriet in, shall we say three months.'

'Otherwise, I think she will be quite well with you, but please don't hesitate to contact us, should you become concerned in the meantime.'

He drew her closer towards him now, with the pretence of confidentiality. Her perfume was quite magical, it drifted towards him in soft undulating waves. A summer's afternoon in the harsh of winter. He pictured her briefly with her hair down in a meadow of violets. He felt poetic.

Grace caught his expression and noted that he had drifted off. Men could be such terribly simple creatures at times, what deadly bores they were. She smiled her second best smile, and tried exceptionally hard to remove the sigh from her eyes.

'There will be some odd behaviour,' he spoke quietly so the girl would not hear, 'she tends to repeat herself and mentions a young girl. We have seen her spend a long time just looking out at the water.'

'Don't worry Doctor, there are two of us, I am a twin you know. She will have the best of care. I understand.'

'Of course, be kind to her, she is still fragile, but I'm sure the love of her family will bring her on in leaps in bounds.'

And with that, the girl in the summer meadow retreated from him and in a fleeting moment he saw her in duplicate, which was quite an extraordinary and splendid thing.

When the call came through for the cab to the station, Jim jumped at the chance. He knew it would be the beautiful woman and he so wanted to see her again, even if just for a moment. It wasn't very often her strong type of beauty was found. On his way over to the Lake House, he fantasised that the train would be delayed and perhaps they would have a cup of tea and a chat. He wasn't stupid, knew that nothing would ever come of it. But it would be nice if people saw him with her and wondered and spoke about it.

Jim could do with some kudos.

He found her with a tight grip on a shorter girl's wrist. This girl's hair was un-brushed, she had been crying recently and she looked right through him. He noticed some scratches and scars on her arms and he at once understood, why the fair woman was a rescuing angel!

There was no time for tea, which disappointed him. They made good time and there was a train due shortly. The women had not spoken in the car. He caught her eye a few times in the mirror and she smiled so sweetly and benignly at him that he couldn't help but be touched.

The slam of the door, the 'let me help you ladies,' the blow of the whistle, the kerrr-clunk, kerr-clunk of the engine slowly picking up speed, the smell of the steam. Oh how he heard and smelt everything about that train so very keenly.

'You all right Jim? Come and have a tea,' said the Station Master.

But he wanted to watch the train until it had rounded the corner and carried them away. Such precious cargo.

They alighted at the platform in the dark, it was still

only early evening, and they had made extraordinary swift progress. Grace looked at the child, who still had not spoken and thought it wise that they didn't walk home, so they called another cab and arrived at the house with the green front door, still under a cover of snow.

Charity had been waiting, she had spent the day watching out of the window and now at long last here they were, everything was in place and that was such a great relief.

'Nearly there.' She said to Mother's portrait.

'Clickedly click, won't be a tick.' She replied.

CHAPTER 33

They put her in her old bedroom and were kind to her that first night. A sandwich and pot of tea were brought up to her on a tray by Charity. There was even a bar of chocolate and a kiss on the top of her head.

Her room was as it was when she left it and that comforted her, there had been no bleaching, they had not changed a thing, except for her bedding which was fresh and clean. This act of kindness had surprised her. She knew it had not been Greta as the first thing she had done was run into that familiar kitchen, calling her name.

The twins had followed her closely behind and slowly shook their heads at her confusion.

'She had to go darling.'

'But…'

Then remembering the peck of the beaks and the cold of the aviary floor, she decided to not discuss it and instead found herself nodding.

'Good girl.'

And with that she made her way up the stairway. She could smell bleach, felt the light despite it being night time – how had they managed to do that? She noticed the cracks all over the celling and saw Mother's face watching her knowingly and with kindness from the painting that still hung in prime position.

'Up the stairs to Bedfordshire my darling.'

She checked the drawers, her kohl was still rolled up hidden in a sock, Pa's waistcoat still hung in her wardrobe. The little bit of money she had 'acquired' was still in her little Wedgewood blue pot.

She slept well in the darkness and the quiet. She couldn't hear the sound of the water here, the waves weren't lapping slowly at the shore which seemed to resonate so loudly and strongly in her head, she had found it quite impossible to sleep. There would be no pointing and calling through the ether by the child tonight.

Bathed in her unquiet.

It was dark when she woke. There was no light creeping around the curtains, surely she couldn't be awake yet?

As if they had just been waiting, the door flung open and there they were, resplendent in white, shining in the darkness.

'You've had a very long sleep dear.'

'Mother always used to say that sometimes this is just what is needed, so we let you rest dear girl.'

'Yes, Mother was quite right, no need to wake until one absolutely has to, do you remember dear how elevenses were usually her breakfast.'

'She was so wise, she asked us to take care of you dear, so we will.'

'She's here darling, she never left.'

'Plenty of time for that later Charity dear.'

'It's time for afternoon tea, a man from the Cadena has brought us pikelets and cake, he hoped they would make you feel a little better.'

'Ten minutes, Harriet dear, no need to dress.'

Sitting up in bed she realised she must have slept for about 15 hours, she felt a little clearer, felt the mist starting to leave her, felt the eternal coldness begin to leave her bones. She was wary of her sisters, but she could appreciate that they were trying their best and that Grace had come and brought her home. For now that was better than the cold of the lake and the voices.

A rug had been placed on the sofa in the lounge. Grace sat on the other side and patted the seat next to her.

'Best not get anything grubby, eh.'

'What do you mean dear, I was hoping that the rug would warm you, we do need to take care you know?'

A fire had been lit, it had a lovely warming glow and she could smell herbs gently glowing in the heat, a lovely botanical woodiness, what was it sage, rosemary?

'Sage dear, glorious isn't it, detoxifying apparently.'

As the twins busied themselves with high tea, Charity poring tea from Mothers vast teapot, which she hadn't seen for years, Ted's goodies were placed in front of her, such a delicious treat.

She felt lulled and peaceful for the first time in oh so long.

After eating things that would not have been allowed at the Lake House, too decadent and not conducive to a healthy mind, she felt herself glance around the room.

She could tell that her sisters had taken charge. The once green walls were a pristine bright white, there was an abundance of paintings on display, including the birds which if she sat at a certain angle, didn't trouble her line of vision.

The house seemed in a worse state of repair than ever with more and more cracks, but the whiteness offset it and the girls looked like they belonged. There were flowers and paintings and light - she could see that they were starting again.

They sat companionably for a few hours, Charity sketching on a notepad stretched in front of the fire, in itself an extraordinary thing. There was no rushing up to the attic studio room to be alone. Grace sat quietly reading Dickens, 'stuff and nonsense,' she declared every so often, but didn't put it down. And as for Harriet she simply sat and was amazed at the comfortable scene around her. She couldn't quite believe that the people that had made her life undoubtedly uncomfortable before, were the same women sitting with her now.

'I think perhaps you should rest some more Harriet,' said Charity eventually, putting down her sketchpad. Harriet saw a picture of Milly the cat.

'Milly?'

'Yes dear, she seems to have gone on her travels, I'm sure she will return home now you are here.'

'Perhaps she is with Greta.'

'Perhaps dear, wherever that is.'

With that Grace snapped up her book, 'bath time Harriet, cleanliness is next to Godliness as you know and we mustn't allow any germs to settle in.'

'We have done so very well at cleaning them up so far' said Charity.' It would be a terrible shame if an infection took hold again.'

'Zip, zappity zap.'

And suddenly all the bon homine left the room, all of them remembering that Christmas, only a few months, yet a lifetime ago.

They had not altered so much.

She was scrubbed until red and the Dettol stung her skin and the fumes made her cough. She was indeed very clean. There were no tears this time, she let them do it to her, it was easier now that there was no resistance.

A clean white nightie had been found from somewhere, which was slipped over her head, it smelt of bleach too and with a kiss on her forehead from both of them, she went back to bed.

Her dreams were of the lake house and the water dripped into her mind that night. Suddenly she was there struggling through the water, Unity just a never ending few paces in front of her, no matter how far she swam, how she tried to reach her.

It was so realistic, she felt the water fall into her eyes, droplets on her skin. Willing herself to open her eyes for the nightmare to stop, it was with a cold terror that she saw the back of a man at the foot of her bed, arms raised muttering strange words in the darkness.

Screaming now, her eyes adjusting to the light in the room, she saw the girls at the end of the bed sitting on chairs watching her quietly, smiling.

'Continue, please do.'

Pinned to the spot in sheer terror, she watched him turn to face her, dressed in black, she first noticed the bottle in his hand – what was this?

He flung the bottle towards her, water or something falling all over her and she looked down at her nightdress and saw spots of water making the gown translucent in places. In horror she grabbed the covers around her, but he was quicker than she was and he held her fast, whilst more water was poured over her.

'Thank you, Vicar.'

'At last, we truly have her back.'

He stepped away after he had placed his hands unnecessarily on her body, her nakedness now showing through the wet nightdress. She felt him linger longer on certain parts of her. Harriet lay rigid in shock. It was a position she was becoming all the more used to.

'Well done my dear.'

'They'll be no more nasty dreams.'

Then the three of them left.

Once they'd gone, she ran to her chest of drawers and pushed with the little strength she had left so that it blocked the door. Once she was safely ensconced in her room, the tears finally fell, the pent-up tears that had waited so long, finally purged in a choking, spluttering outpouring of fear and frustration. She tore away at the nightgown and put on one of Father's big moth balled smelling shirts, which reached her knees.

'Oh Pa.'

Wrapping herself in her blanket, she finally cried herself to sleep. It was the collapse of the defeated, those at battle. An empty and dead sleep, which her family knew so well.

Three days later and relationships were decidedly frosty.

'Darling girl, we had to help you.'

'That place, the girl, surely they have left you now?'

Harriet couldn't deny it, she had, had no more dreams of Unity and the Lake House was leaving her, she could feel it losing its tenacious hold.

'You didn't have to do that.'

'Ssh dear, eat.'

They were feeding her up again, trying to nurture her. They spend their evenings in front of the fireplace and to an outsider it was a scene of familial comfort. But Harriet had lost what little trust she had left.

'How do you know about the child?'

'Dear, we know more than you can ever imagine… and that is why we have had to do what we have.'

Harriet had asked to leave the house a number of times, she was desperate to find Tustin, desperate for some real affection. She missed her friend Greta but most of all she needed to talk to her brother.

'Not yet dear, the weather is still chilly and you are in recovery.'

'Don't make us have to send you back to the Lake House.'

And with that threat lingering in the air, Harriet did the best she could and bided her time.

She went into Guy's study, the place she had sat with him on so many evenings. The key was in the usual place and she unlocked the cabinet with that delphinium blue ribbon and took the 'medicine' upstairs. She knew what it could do, she didn't touch a drop herself, but she looked at it and wondered if she would ever have to use it again. It gave her some security that things could never get too bad, because if they did, she could take a drink and escape.

Harriet also went into his money box, which was still there, full of notes. She took that too, she didn't bother to hide what she had done, felt that her siblings were the very last people to comment on (in the grand scheme of things) such a small misdemeanour. It sat next to the laudanum and those two items represented a freedom, she was yet to fully discover.

'We were right to let her find it,' said Grace.

'Bolster the spirits a little,' said Charity.

She liked the new room though, the candles had gone, the worn tatty lampshades disappeared, it too was white and paintings that the girls had produced adorned the walls. They were cheerful flower scenes, quite a departure from some of their work. A gold frame with a photograph of their mother sat on the desk. It can't have been long before she died. She was just the way Harriet remembered her. She sat for a long time just looking at it.

'She loved you very much dear.'

'What does that matter now Charity, she's dead.'

Charity smiled at her quite benignly and let her be.

. . .

Greta had also been spending long days simply staring into space. It was difficult for her to get her thoughts into any order.

They were mostly quite kind to her, but now they had discovered she was German, some of the staff were less than helpful. One orderly kept accidently spilling drinks and the like onto her and gave her noticeably smaller portions of food. But they weren't all like that and she had recently gone through so much worse, it didn't trouble her. She even felt like she deserved it.

It reminded her a little of recovering from the Spanish flu. It was terrible, but she'd been through the worst of it.

But still the thoughts would not line up, there was no chronology of events and no timeline that made any sense.

'It is the fever, who knows the effect that has had, we will only know with time, so try not to let it distress you,' said doctor, after nurse, after specialist.

She remembered the evening of the New Year's Eve party. There they all were in that now unrecognisable house. She had fallen in love with Guy and for once there was the possibility of a future, of something other than being a cook and companion and cleaner. And she had been radiant, she had even made those little broches and presents for them all. It seemed so very long ago. No matter how hard she tried, she couldn't remember what had led her to this place in such a very short space of time.

She had 'talking therapy' at Hatton. They took her on a bus with other quiet troubled folk. She quite enjoyed the drive out into the countryside, past the fields and the emerging spring flowers in the hedgerows. She could see animals grazing on the land. It was a trip away. She didn't even mind the big imposing building that greeted her at the end of her bus journey. It was like any other hospital she had been in and the people she met smiled at her as they took her into the room.

'Now let's try and remember Greta.'

'Did anyone hurt you?'

'Where were you living?'

'Do you have any family?'

She pretended that she didn't know the answer to the questions, the last thing in the world she wanted was to be returned to that building and those women.

But she couldn't remember where Harriet or Guy had gone, what on earth had happened?

They had started to speak about electronic therapy if there was no improvement, she had heard about this and hoped it wouldn't come to that as she didn't want to lose what little of her memory she had left.

After a few weeks, fragments started to appear in her mind and as they grew in their ferocity she began to long for the treatment, anything to make it go away.

But the benign people in their white coats were having none of that now.

Greta was once again at the party and she saw herself laughing with Guy, she remembered she had drunk champagne. She looked at the young lovers, Harriet and Tustin, so very obvious, so beautiful. She watched Guy watch them too, was it with the same affection? Could a brother wish that for a sister, she didn't know. Still it was a glorious evening and she was spun round the room giggling. People were surprised that Guy was so familiar with 'staff' as they saw it. He didn't care, in fact she thought he rather enjoyed the rebellion of it and she loved him a little bit more for that.

A fragment of her outside in the cold on the doorstep, unsure what to do, confused, torn.

Then Harriet, cold and shivering with her. They'd moved further down the street at this point, why on earth had they done that? She was sobbing violently.

'It's fine liebling.'

'All is well, all is well.'

What was that in her hands? She saw a bottle a number of times but could quite ascertain what it was. On waking she told her mind to study it again in her sleep, which was a technique they had given her at the hospital. Still it would not come.

There was Harriet drinking whatever was inside and then more confusion, more crying and then suddenly as clear as anything, as clear as the day itself, she watched herself in her beautiful new party dress walk away, back towards the house, onto the threshold, opening the door and stepping inside. All without looking back once and leaving her. LEAVING HER in the snow and the cold on that night of all nights.

The fever returned shortly after she had remembered this and they put her all alone in a side ward, and the people that did come and see her were only allowed in wearing masks.

The twins were right, there was dis-ease.

Once the fever had passed, she asked to see a priest. She had a renewed sense of purpose, she had to find the girl and explain. Did the twins know? No wonder they hadn't turned her out on the street immediately when they had found Harriet's poor body grasping onto life.

She had seen her once in the hospital, bloodied and torn. Had sat with her for hours holding her hand tightly. The twins crossly looking on. Harriet was unaware she was even there, did Greta even know at that moment what she had done? She couldn't have done as she remembered feeling cross with the twins for being standoffish even as she lay there in a hospital bed and needed so much love and care. Then all too soon she had gone, been taken somewhere, she couldn't remember where to recover. What had she done? The one person she loved and truly cared for, it made no sense.

She couldn't remember when the fever had started, when she fell so ill at the house. Was it her night in the cold, or the guilt? The obvious wracking and most terrible guilt that had done it. No wonder her clever mind did its best to forget.

Greta wasn't a very religious woman, too much had happened for that and yet she began to pray, as much for the woman she thought she was, but so evidently wasn't, as for Harriet herself.

Greta discharged herself sometime later. The benign people in the white coats didn't want her to go, they wanted her to go to relatives that they didn't know didn't exist.

Greta left the town, it wasn't right for her to be there at this moment, she needed to gather herself together. She took another bus ride into the beautiful Warwickshire countryside. She had heard of Hunningham, if she remembered rightly, Tustin had a connection. There was a pub on the banks of the river and she worked for her lodging. They hadn't wanted her to serve in case people realised she was a German, but they let her clean and wash up. It was tiring work, but it gave her purpose and it felt only fitting that she should endure some hardships.

After a few weeks, she stepped onto the bus again, passed trees, sheep and little sleepy villages. Spring had sprung in abundance, daffodils, crocuses and sunshine managing to streak their way through the clouds.

She walked to the park, the picture was still not entirely clear. She sat and forced herself to look at the aviary, that most awful of places. But no memories came to her of that snowy night. After some time, Greta walked through the gates and a glimpse of Harriet's bare arm and hand clutching at the wrought iron arrived in her mind. She shook her head, but it was definitely her hand, the little heart ring that her mother had given her that was always on her finger, shining out as a signal in the moonlight.

Stealing herself she walked through those gates and was faced with the sight of the house, could she do it? Would she be brave enough? A deep breath and pushing away of thoughts of her in her nightgown in the snow, the bloodied trail she left; of Harriet in her evening dress, whiteness falling all around them both. On her mouth in the sunshine she could taste the icy flakes.

Greta knocked on that door and was greeted with silence. Knocked again, still nothing. She stood there, unsure of what to do. She hadn't prepared for nothingness, she was geared up to meet them, to ask questions, action, anything but the quiet.

Looking out of the Newbold Arms window, for the first time in days, a sorry thin figure thought he saw someone on his doorstep. It couldn't be? He took a sip of the last of his medicine, gasping at the dregs and looked again. He was convinced.

There was no time to look respectable. He sprayed the cheap aftershave over himself to mask the worst of him and munched frantically through the mints he always had as a precaution. He swiped his hands through his hair and hoped his overcoat would hide a multitude of sins and swept from the room. She was already walking back towards the park by the time he made it outside. His lungs complained of the air, the shock of the fresh and his eyes spontaneously watered. Wiping the moisture away he hurried after her.

'Excuse me madam,' he tapped her on the shoulder.

In the time it took her to turn around, he managed to gather his breath.

'It can't be, Guy?'

She stumbled a little and grabbed at his arm.

'Let me help you, would you like some tea?'

He said it matter of factly, as if it was the most normal thing in the world.

He steered her back to those gates, 'oh no not again.' She was too faint now to complain and as they pushed through, she saw that ringed hand again disembodied on the gate post.

Past the aviary, past the clock tower, past the swans

that used to cheer her up and into the café that just a short time ago had made her feel so positive.

'My dear you look pale.'

He pulled out a seat and sat and studied her face, did she even remember?

They ate cake in silence, Greta choked it back, felt it sticking in her throat, it felt impossible. Guy of course had no interest in cake and he toyed with it. They both acted the part they knew they had to play out.

'Are the twins well?'

He asked the question so casually, it confused her.

'At the house my dear, is all well?'

She drifted to a dark street on a moonlit night and the inky black enveloped her momentarily.

'I don't live there anymore Guy.'

'My dear, but I saw you on the steps, just now. Are you un-well?'

He had to pinch himself, he had seen her hadn't he, on the steps? And he was here having tea and infernal cake with her, wasn't he? It wasn't one of 'the others'? How could you eat cake with the others? It was impossible.

'Oh Guy, it's been so very long.'

And with that she took his hand and she noticed its thinness, saw the confusion, saw the watery eyes and she knew he was that lost boy again and with it her heart gave way a little and she felt even more lost. Didn't know what to do. So, they sat there in silence, Greta keeping his hand in hers.

'Time to leave Sir and Madam.'

They stood up now, and Greta had no idea how ten minutes later she was sitting on the end of a bed in a small dark room. In her hands was a glass, in the glass was a thick viscose liquid. He sat behind her, she felt his arms on her, he enveloped her, and she felt his breath on her neck.

'It's OK, I'll take care of you.'

And with those words, she drank, what else was she meant to do?

He held her fast whilst the whiteness came. It moved in waves inside of her. So, this is what it feels like. Oblivion. It was goodness and light and hope all rolled into one.

She grew to enjoy it, she flew, saw her spirit soar, floated in the undulating clouds that cosseted her, buffered her ever so gently. And that was the key.

It was, oh so ever so.

Oh, so ever so became quite the habit and she surprised herself on a daily basis. In order to be oh so ever so, required at times levels of cunning she was unaware she possessed. They fought often, and he had started to call her 'Cheri' sometimes. At first, she tried to tell herself it was an affectionate 'dear' and not the name of the dead wife.

Then the cosseting clouds came and she didn't mind one bit.

And they watched, for hours, the big white house with the now white door. If they did ever see the door open or the twins outside, they had absolutely zero energy to move.

'Guy, we should go now and talk to them.'

'Harriet, I need to see my liebling frau.'

But the thoughts, as all her thoughts, ebbed and flowed eventually away before they could be grasped, let alone actioned upon.

'She was so cold Guy, out there alone in the snow.'

'We did the right thing. It was the only thing my dear.'

'We didn't do that, did we Guy, not us, surely not?'

'We helped her my little Cheri, did what any loving parents would do.'

And even within her befuddled mind, she knew he was lost again. 'She's your sister Guy, your sister.'

'Always the good girl, always my girl.'

And with that they both slept, long with violet and delphinium dreams.

Over a breakfast of cold toast and fractured egg and disappointment at one in the afternoon, the new barmaid asked Greta if she'd like a walk around the park before her shift started.

'Thank you, but I couldn't possibly, I've work to do.'

'Dear Greta,' Guy reached across the table and clasped her hand quite tightly, which would be another mark to try and conceal later she thought.

'You must go and embrace the season, spring is here, I'm sure of it.'

As she resisted again, Guy found himself becoming more insistent which surprised him immensely, he was quite enjoying having her back again, back in their flat with the sounds of the sea. He dug his nails into her wrist to make sure she understood that he needed some time alone and eventually she acquiesced. He did so hope that she wasn't going to become tiresome. Women were often so troublesome.

'Well I'd love to then, thank you Deborah.'

When they reached the park gates, she saw Harriet's young little hand on the wrought iron again and had a little stumble.

'Come on deary, I think you really need this fresh air today.' Deborah was sweet and seemed a little concerned about her, for which she had no reason why. Wasn't she living the dream, cosied away with the man she loved?

She glanced backwards and could see that terrible house in the corner of her eye and there she was in the hallway, Guy kissing her neck and she felt emboldened as if the whole of the world was suddenly at her feet. It was going to be a wonderful New Year.

'I don't think we're the only lovers tonight are we dear?'

He knew, he'd seen the powder too, so she giggled at a wonderful shared confidence.

'It is a night for magic.'

Had she really said that, it seemed rather ridiculous now. She saw Charity watching them from the lounge room and she wasn't smiling or laughing or looking gay.

It seemed to make the conspiratorial nature of her and Guy's relationship somehow more appealing and thrilling. She felt like she was in a romance novel and she hadn't felt anything close to that for a long while.

'I think I should really talk to her alone, don't you? Check she's all right, wouldn't want any old chap to get in the way.'

What a strange choice of words that seems now, but at the time she didn't think so, nothing else registered but his arm around her and his whispering voice. Nothing else mattered or was important.

'Hard as it is to drag myself away from you,' and she heard herself giggle in quite a surprising whimsical way. Oh, it had been so terribly easy. Who was this woman acting like a simpering child? She tried to put the thoughts to one side as Deborah was getting a little annoyed with her too now.

'Come on missey, stop staring into space, I think we might need some tea,' and there she was being moved along, quite gently towards the aviary, the only way to the tea shop.

'Have a little nip, it's good for the soul.' And it was Guy's smiling face coaxing her, and she felt like a bold woman with a future ahead of her as she took the drink. It burnt her throat and she exclaimed, but it made him kiss her neck very gently as if to soothe its passage and she liked that. Very much.

It was before, 'oh, so ever so.' But it was very 'oh so ever so,' all the same.

'Ask Harriet to meet me outside would you, I'll run on

up to the park gate, don't want the twins to overhear, you know how hard they can be on her, don't want to let the cat out of the bag straight away now do we?'

How they laughed, even as he pressed his little hip flask into her pocket and said, 'Let's treat Harry to a nip too, shall we.'

She didn't make it to the tea shop and slumped down on the nearest bench.

Oh no, no, surely not. He was there. At the park. On that night. And so was she.

'Wake-up Cheri, come along now, don't do this to me again.'

Greta came round to find Guy poking at her and calling that woman's name over and over again.

'You are a child.'

'Mais oui amour, mais oui.'

It was much easier to let him continue and call her what he liked. If she questioned it, it would increasingly trouble and confuse him, and all Greta really wanted at this point was an easier time to gather her thoughts.

It was the way of things now and her new normal.

She knew she should walk away but she also knew that she had to know what had happened and these people were her link to Harriet.

'I should go and fetch her from the beach now my love.'

And with that, he put on his overcoat and hat and left.

Greta rolled over and slept some more.

She awoke to find him sitting on the end of the bed, watching her.

'Her lips are delphinium blue, such a pretty colour Cheri, always so stylish my love. I couldn't find her in the sea, I expect she has found a hidden cove or is playing with the fish, you know how she loves that my dear.'

'Delphinium, all is delphinium.'

They ate a sparse meal of crackers and chocolate and

listened to the wireless. They danced and laughed, and Guy was on the island smelling the orange blossom in her hair.

CHAPTER 34

☀

It was with a marvellous serendipity that the sun shone on the white house with its newly painted white door and on Greta's tired and ravaged face which looked out from the window.

'It is a day full of brightness Grace.' Trilled Charity.

'I shall wear my whites, it is a good day.'

'Charity, let us begin then.' replied Grace.

'Harriet, Harriet,' they called in unison.

They dressed her in their likeness with a little hat to cover her dark hair, they'd sort that out later. It was the best they could do for now.

'Ladies, how may I help you?'

At the department store, their usual server couldn't help but let out a little gasp. He was always bowled over by the magnificent Leighton twins, and now look at the younger sister! A beauty too, how she had grown.'

They placed their order and smiled their most marvellous smiles, just to see him blush and stumble. What japes!

'Well done Harriet, Mother would be so terribly proud.'

'As a reward, we'll take you to that unusual little place you are so strangely fond of.'

'Good idea Charity, replied Grace, we must of course also thank them for their kindness of the pikelets and cake.'

'Well, that's what us Leighton girls must do, keep up the families reputation.'

Harriet hadn't failed to notice, the effect her new appearance was having on Leamington Spa. They were stopped often, people asked how she was and how tremendous she looked. She was ashamed to admit that it gave her a little thrill.

'Dazzle and shine my loves.'

'My good God' muttered Ted as they graced the Cadena. He instantly warmed up and had to excuse himself for five minutes whilst he composed himself and let out a little laugh.'

'That's my girl alright.'

They ate pikelets and drank tea as was the custom. Ted put them in the window seat so everyone could see them at his establishment.

He took a chance to brush past Harriet's leg and all three women turned towards him with the most devasting smiles. He stumbled backwards. It was as simple as that.

'Devastate them with your deliciousness.'

The door opened with a ting-a-ling-ling and there stood Greta, who bolted upright with a ping.

'Liebling!'

Three faces looked, but none of them smiled or even acknowledged the drawn looking woman standing in front of them.

'More tea, dear?'

'Thanks Grace,' said Harriet and smiled the Leighton girl smile at her sister.

'Harriet, it's me Greta, your friend.'

'Jam, dear?'

And with that a shocked Greta left and ran all the way

back to her new home.

On their return the twins decided to reward Harriet for her good behaviour.

'Dear girl, do you remember when you chopped off your hair? We found one of those Hollywood magazines in your wastepaper bin and there was that actress with the pale hair.'

'Jean Harlow, Grace,' said a bemused Harriet, wondering where on earth this was heading towards.

'The very same, I thought she looked rather beautiful, didn't you?'

'Well yes, but Guy really wouldn't like my hair that way.'

'These things are never the concern of menfolk my dear. As Mother used to say, be bold and brave.'

'Grace, what a tremendous idea, shall we all throw a little caution to the wind. Leighton girls forward!' chimed in Charity.

'You mean, I can actually do it?' Harriet couldn't quite believe her luck.

'Not you dear, but we can do it for you, no time like the present, snip snap!'

And for once Harriet willingly let her sisters pour bleach over her head until it was as white as white. Finally, she had her film star peroxide bob. How she wished she could share her new look with her friends and maybe even take a trip to the clock tower. With her new found look she felt renewed, even hopeful.

'You see darling girl, we'll make everything better.'

And three blonde sisters stood in front of Mother, resplendent and glowing with light.

'That's my girls.'

CHAPTER 35

The next morning, Harriet awoke to a familiar tune, and before she knew it was singing along.

'Happy days are here again, the skies above are clear again…'

Mother's tune, the one she played incessantly up to that final terrible night.

She heard Grace in the room next door;

'Your care's and troubles are gone; they'll be no more from now on.'

And then before she could stop herself, Harriet saw Guy, wriggling away from Mother's grasp and leaving her room that night. His eyes red and sore, Mother calling out for her 'dear little pansy.'

It made her feel undeniably uncomfortable.

Charity had joined in now too. 'Happy, happy days are here again!'

They ate breakfast served on the duck egg china plates and planned another excursion.

'Let's show the world a united front shall we.'

'Perhaps a little walk in the park, do you think you are able Harriet? Shall we try very hard to banish some demons?'

Reluctantly Harriet agreed. At least in the park she was

near the clock tower and the bridge as well, and all that, that meant. She would at some point have to walk past the aviary and it may as well be today.

'As long as we are all together.'

They made a striking contingent as they walked past their white house, with the newly white front door and onwards the short distance to the park. Anyone they met, immediately nodded in a peculiar kind of deference, they had that air about them. It hung around them like Channel no.5.

Poouf! Once released in the ether, there wasn't a vaccine alive that could cure anyone of the Leighton girls.

As they approached the gates Harriet paused, trying desperately to replace the nightmare-ish visions with memories of Tustin. The twins held her up in the middle.

'We are Leighton girls, we can do anything,' said a firm Charity.

She saw her brother walking her into the park that night.

'What did you do?' Harriet said quietly.

The twins looked at each other.

'As we expected.'

They continued there slow and stately progress.

At the clock tower they paused, and Harriet even managed a weak smile.

'You'll meet him again soon dear heart, when you are better.' said Grace.

'Thank you,' again, quietly.

Behind the clock tower lay the aviary and it knocked some of the air out of her chest to see it, but feeling more and more emboldened by her new found 'Leighton-ness' on they proceeded and took a seat opposite that most terrible of spaces.

She saw her brother in that enclosed vile space. He was dancing in the corner watching her, throwing violets in the air.

A little girl walked past that seemed strangely familiar. She turned around and Harriet knew that little face anywhere. She turned to smile and waved before skipping onwards and far away.

Harriet raised her hand in reply and noticed that her sisters were also waving into the ether, into the nothingness, into the violet empty space.

'What did he do?'

'You know now my dear?'

'We think he is not quite himself.'

'He hasn't been for, oh so very long.'

'But, I thought he loved me.' And Harriet found she was sobbing.

'Yes, maybe a little too much, my dear. He had that about him.'

'Madly and jealously, I think you became her, his second chance.'

'Unity?'

'Yes, he loved her very much didn't he, she's been showing us the way for quite a while now.'

'Sustenance,' said Charity and they arose in triplicate and walked away from that terrible place.

'So much more valuable than a month in that confounded Lake House,' whispered Grace.

'Indeed, my dear, indeed.'

'But it gave us the space to make the necessary arrangements.'

They had a pot of tea and jam doughnuts, and all three seemed a little brighter and a little less burdened. Harriet could not help but be reminded of Greta, her friend and companion who had so often sat in front of her with a pot of tea just as they were doing now.

'And, Greta?'

'She was infected my dear, couldn't quite help from being tainted.'

'We needed to cleanse whilst we could, do you

understand?'

'Mother advised it of course, she always did show such sound judgement.'

'I thought… the birds, why did you draw so many?'

'Attention to detail my girl, one must be meticulous to succeed.'

'And our little home is safe now.'

It is clean.

CHAPTER 36

Back at the lodgings, Guy and Greta awoke after another restless night. Greta had sat and listened to Guy mumbling about his mother, asking her to stop holding him so tightly and he woke screaming; 'leave me be, leave me be.'

In a half awaking he was asking her to leave the child alone, and; 'must you have another drink now Mother?'

In the white house with the newly white front door, Harriet had also had a dream. Guy was running out of Mother's room crying again and she ran to her big brother and held his hand. It reminded her of all those nights they'd spent together whilst he had his special medicine.

She missed him, but it wasn't that straightforward now.

Her sisters, ever watchful, had seen him too.

Harriet remembered that later that evening, her mother had asked for a special drinkie and she'd popped some medicine in. She had only done what she'd seen her mother do in the past. It quietened Mama and they'd slept cuddled up together until that last morning.

Mother smelt of Channel no.5, powder and violets.

Hermione Lucretia Leighton, née Codrington didn't wake-up ever again.

And then she had remembered another part of another terrible night. There was Guy standing in the middle of the aviary, he whipped up the birds into such a frenzy, and she heard him say:

'Well, Mother, you've enjoyed another little dalliance this evening, haven't you?'

'The dalliances must stop, must desist.'

'There will be no more violets.'

'I must do this my dear, I must.'

Grace had also had a troubled night, which was most unusual for her.

The girls rarely had trouble sleeping. They told themselves it was because they were so in tune with the moon and the stars and the universe.

She also went back to that night and saw Guy leave Mother, his eyes red with tears, it could not have been a coincidence that the next morning she had died.

She had seen the relief on her brother's face, he hadn't been quick enough to hide it. He was on a visit back from France, he knew of death and such things. It had to be.

He was the infection.

Mother had chosen the wrong special little man, hadn't she?

As she peeled her sister from those dead arms the next morning, she swore to keep him at a distance and be watchful over this motherless little thing.

They had slipped up that night of the party, the house had been unforgiving. Grace and Charity wouldn't let that happen again.

They had frequently cleansed their sister, to curb the monstrous tenacious infection that was threatening to take hold. They had kept it at bay even with the disease living with them.

Leighton girls do not allow poison to take hold.

'Drop-kick it into submission darlings,' Mother instructed as often as she could.

The house was how it should be now. Finally, after all their hard work they could enjoy it and prepare themselves for the end.

'Illuminate not dissipate.'

RESURECTION

🔥 ✿ 🔥

And so it was, that two weeks later Guy received an invitation to tea.

'Ha!' 'Fools!'

But, at the prescribed time, he made himself look as presentable as possible, picked up some white lilies and presented himself at the white door.

'Do come into our home brother.'

He noted the intonation and kissed his three sisters on the cheek. He gasped when he saw Harriet's transformation and she at his.

'Was it me?' He whispered in her ear.

'Violet ghosts,' she responded.

'I thought so, they are everywhere.'

Harriet held his hand as she led him into the lounge. His old study was unrecognisable and he applauded his sisters at their coup de force.

'Bravo sisters, bravo.'

Charity carried the tray of tea, as Guy went to reach for his cup, he noticed a familiar key with a pretty blue delphinium key.

'Please, we've no need of this.'

Guy took the key and walked over to his old desk, now painted white. His favoured glass was there and he poured a very large measure of his medicine into it.

It went down very well with the Victoria Sponge as Harriet held his hand.

The clocks ticked, lips were licked, cake crumbs were picked, soon limbs kicked as they fell into a sleep that he'd been missing.

'It's time now little bird,' he said once again to his little sister.

Mother smiled at him from the photograph on the table.

'Sleepy time little pansy boy, sleepy night time.'

The sisters left him in the big white house with the newly white door.

'Should I blow out the candles?' asked Harriet.

'Let's not disturb him dear, they will simply dissolve.'

'There is someone waiting for you, best not disappoint them now dear.'

As Harriet stepped out onto the threshold, a fresh breeze caught her, intoxicating her. Spring jasmine and lime trees.

She took a deep breath and closed her eyes and walked passed Harrington House with its fairy tale turrets and onto the park gates.

There he was waiting for her outside the clock tower. The gates opened all by themselves. It was the same yet a world away.

As an early spring evening turned to dusk, the girls enjoyed their moonlight dancing around the house. Mother kissed them lightly twice on each cheek, as was the fashion.

Guy slept a sleep full of delphinium dreams.

'The ultimate cleanse, the purest slayer of disease will soon be upon us sister.'

'It is the only way things can start again.'

'Up the wooden stairs to Bedfordshire, my little ones,' coaxed Mother one last time.

...

The flames lapped testily around their cool white bodies, afraid of the brightness, of the cold. But they soon began to enjoy the new sensation and languidly and lovingly licked at the bodies that offered no resistance.

'Mother does prefer a live flame.'

And before long they were iridescent in their absolute whiteness.

Bathed in violet, bathed in the beginning.

AUTHOR'S NOTES

Leamington Spa is my home town. The town I grew up in. It's where I first kissed boys in parks, danced, wrote & painted.

As far as I'm aware there isn't a room in the clock tower in the park (but I wish there were!)

Harrington house is no longer, nor is the aviary. It used to make me tremble when I was a little girl to see the birds all shut up. I'm pleased that's long gone.

My family have a tradition of shimmying up the beautiful blue bridge, but they've put bins there now, so that isn't so easy anymore!

Many of the locations are special to me and still exist. You can find them if you like!

I apologise for any historical inaccuracies, many moments are simply taken from my mind and have no base in fact.

I hope you enjoy this tale as much as I enjoyed creating it. Thank you for getting this far and supporting me.

♥

Printed in Great Britain
by Amazon